WILD

T

WILD

Koala Crazy!

LUCY COURTENAY

First published in Great Britain in 2012
by Hodder Children's Books

1

A Catalogue record for this book is available from the British Library

ISBN 978 1 444 90986 9

Typeset in AGaramond by Avon DataSet Ltd,
Bidford on Avon, Warwickshire

Printed and bound by
CPI Group (UK) Ltd, Croydon, CR0 4YY

The paper and board used in this paperback by Hodder Children's Books
are natural recyclable products made from wood grown in
sustainable forests. The manufacturing processes conform to the
environmental regulations of the country of origin.

Hodder Children's Books
a division of Hachette Children's Books
338 Euston Road, London NW1 3BH
An Hachette UK company
www.hachette.co.uk

For Sadie

**With special thanks to Chris Brown of Tooth 'n' Claw
and Duncan Bolton of Birdworld.**

1

Hiking to Australia for Real

I practically pushed Joe Morton out of the way to get the first view of the Wild World wildlife park as the school coach swung around the corner. School trips are always exciting – at least *I* think so – but this one was up there, top of the wishlist etc.

'Get your head out of the way, will you, Joe?' I demanded, raising my voice so I would be heard over the racket in the back of the coach, where Tosh and Jonno were trying to swing on the overhead lockers. 'You're hogging the window. I want to see!'

'Blimey, Taya.' Joe pressed himself against the back of his seat so I could lunge across his lap and put my hands on the window and press my nose to the glass. 'Anyone would think you'd never been here before.'

Joe doesn't normally do irony, or even jokes. I pulled an 'OK, so I'm mildly amused' face at him and he looked completely delighted.

You see, I *had* been here before. I'd been here just this morning, eating my toast and listening to the grunts and roars of my animal neighbours. I'd walked down the path from our little white house, past the tigers, past the chimps, past the café and the gift shop and Charlie-on-the-gate, toast crumbs still on my chin (so my twin sister Tori informed me, but not till halfway into school on the bus, which was pretty mean of her – mind you, knowing Tori, she probably genuinely didn't notice). I actually *lived* here. Mum fosters baby animals for the park when their mothers die or get sick, and we live on site so she's always on call. Awesome, right? Plus Dad's a wildlife photographer who runs a business called Wild About Animals, organizing animals for films and adverts. All this *and* 'Wild' for a surname! It's surprising that Tori and I don't have tails and whiskers.

'You'd think Taya'd never been here before!' Joe repeated down the bus, because he was so pleased with the joke he'd somehow made.

The coach hit a pothole and lurched, knocking

me away from the window and straight into Joe's startled lap.

'Taya Wild's sitting on Joe Morton's knee!' squealed Heather Cashman, a couple of seats further back. 'Taya, is Joe your boyfriend?'

She and her mate Carrie Taylor howled at this spectacularly witty and hilarious question – not. Joe blushed as red as a clown's nose.

'Shut up, Heather,' I muttered, sitting down in my own seat as the heat of embarrassment rose up the back of my neck.

'Ooooh! *Boyfriend!*' shrieked Carrie, which made Heather Cashman laugh even harder.

From the seat across the way, Tori looked up from where she was poring over some black-and-white cartoons in an ancient *Doctor Who* annual from the Middle Ages.

'Dawn,' said Tori in her best wildlife-documentary voice, 'and the animals in the jungle are stirring. The Cash 'n' Carrie hyenas are on the prowl. The Jonno and Tosh chimpanzees are—'

There was a crash at the back of the bus, and a yell. We craned our necks to see Tosh's feet waving in the air as he and Jonno lay tangled in a heap in the middle of the aisle.

'—falling out of the trees,' Tori continued.

Cash 'n' Carrie, who'd both looked angry at being compared to hyenas, now decided to laugh thanks to Tori's perfectly timed crack. The rest of the bus joined in. Laughter is amazing stuff. It should be bottled and then released on battlefields and in riots. The trouble would stop dead every time.

'Jonathan Nkobe!' Ms Hutson, our form teacher, bellowed over the hilarity. 'Toshiro Jones! If I weren't going grey already . . .'

'Cheers, Tor,' I said with a grateful glance at my sister for deflecting Cash 'n' Carrie so successfully.

Tori shrugged. 'Thank those comedy chimps at the back of the coach, not me.' She turned to her neighbour, offering her the annual. 'Do you want a look now, Caz?'

Cazza Turnbull always looks like she's preparing to murder the next person who talks to her. But she's OK in a strangely terrifying way, with her death motif badges, regular detentions and insanely illegal school shoes. Tori can't help being a *Doctor Who* obsessive – I think she was born with the Tardis genetically imprinted on her brain – but despite being the coolest and hardest person in Year Seven, Cazza's somehow a *Doctor Who* nerd as well. What are the

4

chances? So the two of them are mates and my sister can count on the Human Timebomb having her back at all times. Lucky cow.

Today Cazza had been scarier than normal, getting into trouble in almost every class. She shook her head furiously at Tori now, then slumped back down in her seat with her earphones on loud and stared out of the window like she was trying to melt the glass with her eyes. The only bit of the journey where she'd perked up was when we passed Inkredible, a tattoo and piercing parlour with the sort of window display designed to give you nightmares for the rest of your life, if needles aren't your thing.

'What's up with . . . ?' I nodded in Cazza's direction.

'Fighting with her mum last night,' Tori told me.

I wondered if Mrs Turnbull still had all her limbs. But I didn't have time to follow this thought any further as the coach swung into the Wild World coach park and the afternoon's fun began.

Jonno and Tosh stayed unusually quiet for much of the way round the park – possibly because whenever they opened their mouths, someone made chimp noises at them so they closed them again. I, on the other hand, couldn't stop talking from the minute the coach stopped and we streamed past Charlie-on-the-gate.

When we started at Forrests I'd got my knickers in a twist about people thinking our life with animals was weird, but I was *wrong*. In fact, it was fantastic, the way half the class was hanging on my words as we walked around – even the ones who'd been here with us a few times, like Joe and our other friend Biro. If my plans to be an actress/fashion designer/singer don't work out, perhaps I'll be a teacher or a politician or some other kind of person who talks a lot and impresses people, because I'm pretty good at it.

'. . . Sinbad the male tiger was born here. He roars in the morning like you wouldn't believe. He's like Mr Jones, our French teacher, on a bad day, only furrier. And the chimps are so unbelievably cute. Grandpa – that's what we named the baby one in there – is getting really big and cheeky now. He threw a rotten banana at one of the keepers at the weekend and laughed. Seriously, he did actually laugh! And you've got to see Ivana the bear; you've probably heard about her riding a bike—'

'Does your sister have an off-button?' Cazza snarled at Tori.

'Nope,' said Tori.

'—and of course Mum's fostered loads of animals since we were really tiny. We had two tiger cubs last term before we moved to Wild World – I expect you heard about that too? You need a Dangerous Wild Animals licence to keep animals like tigers, you know. But we've never had anything Mum couldn't cope with, even though some of the animals we kept were actually seriously dangerous, and we handled them and everything. Like most things, as long as you're sensible nothing bad happens like you being eaten or problems like that.'

'Getting eaten is definitely a problem,' said Tori.

A couple of the girls who'd been listening to me and looking interested giggled at that. I frowned at my twin. There was a time and a place for wisecracks.

'Get a move on, 7H!' called Ms Hutson. 'It's one o'clock already and we haven't reached the marsupial enclosure yet. I feel as if we're hiking to Australia for real.'

We were doing a project on Australia at the moment, so a trip to the world-renowned marsupial enclosure at Wild World completely hit the spot. We were armed with the class camera and drawing pads and quiz sheets, and the plan was for us to do a massive wall display that would give the same effect as walking through the bush to the sound of a didgeridoo, only quieter.

There were a few moans of complaint at this little reminder that we were here on school time, but we all speeded up a bit. Cazza plugged into her iPod again. I listened in a distracted kind of way, trying to work out from the thump-thump-thump exactly what she was listening to. It didn't take long because his music's mega-famous. I opened my mouth to comment.

'New 2thi download, Caz?' said Heather Cashman, beating me to it. 'Awesome.'

'Who's Toothy?' asked Tori.

Cash 'n' Carrie both looked at my sister in disbelief. My own personal jaw was somewhere round my bellybutton. The volume of Caz's iPod was so loud that she wouldn't have heard a stampede of elephants just then, let alone my sister's hideously embarrassing question, so she totally failed to react.

'Am I supposed to have heard of it?' asked Tori, looking at the expressions around her.

'Him, Tor,' I said in an agony of shame. '2thi's a *him*.'

2

As Funny As Measles

I *really* wish my twin would keep her nerdy bits under control in public every now and again. It's not that much to ask. Because we look completely identical with our long brown hair and pale freckly faces, people assume we think and act the same. But we most seriously and absolutely do not. And Tori making confessions like this *does not help*.

Heather looked like an extra Christmas Day had just been delivered into her lap. She and Carrie laughed so hard they had to prop each other up.

'Where's your Tardis, Tori?' Heather choked. 'You'll need it to zoom back to your little nerd planet.'

'Yeah!' squealed Carrie. 'Where's your Tordis, Tari?'

'The Tordis!' gasped Heather in a fresh gust of

laughter. 'Carrie, that's genius. Get it? Tori Wild is *The Tordis*!'

'Course I get it,' said Carrie quickly, like it had been deliberate and not a dim single-brain-cell moment. 'I said it, didn't I?'

'Listen,' I hissed at my sister, frogmarching her away from Cash 'n' Carrie as they howled and shrieked 'TORDIS! TORDIS!' at our backs. Caz followed us, eyes semi shut and head nodding along to her music like a dyed black daffodil in a stiff wind. 'You *have* heard of 2thi the mega-rapper who's won every single award in the world for the last year, Tori. *Everyone's* heard of 2thi.'

'He's a rapper?' Tori asked. 'Don't tell me he spells his name with a number.'

'Duh,' I said. 'Of course he spells it with a number. The number 2. 2-thi. That's the *point*.'

Tori made a gagging noise. She put her hands round her throat, stuck out her tongue and crossed her eyes.

'Are you OK?' I asked in alarm. Was she having some kind of seizure?

Tori lowered her hands. 'That number-name thing is *unbelievably* lame.'

'K9 had a number for a name,' I said. 'You know, the *Doctor Who* dog.'

'Taya, I know who K9 is,' said Tori, 'and it proves my point. K9 as robot dog – fine and actually pretty funny. 2thi as human person – not fine and about as funny as measles. Spelling stuff in stupid ways is just *really* annoying.'

Cazza had taken her earphones out and was now waving them at my twin. 'Wanna listen, Tor?' she offered, in the first flash of a good mood since yesterday. 'Wicked song called "Iz U Iz".'

Ms Hutson loomed out of nowhere, her hand extended in Cazza's direction. 'Give,' she ordered.

Cazza's brief glimmer of good humour disappeared and she looked furious all over again. She handed her iPod over with two or three of her choicest words, which Ms Hutson heroically chose to ignore.

'In case you haven't noticed,' our teacher said, 'we're at the marsupials. We have work to do, 7H!'

The amazing thing about the Wild World marsupial enclosure is that they keep the animals – kangaroos, wallabies, quokkas, wombats and koalas – together in open pasture dotted about with bush-type trees like eucalyptus and tea tree and special Australian daisies and flowers so the animals can feel at home even when the weather is being English, like it most definitely was today. Hopping and trotting about, noses to the ground or in the trees, the marsupials were peacefully snacking their way through the afternoon. The wallabies were perfect miniature versions of the big kangaroos, and the snoozy-looking quokkas were miniature versions of the wallabies, while the fat wombats swayed along with their furry bellies practically touching the ground, and the koalas gripped on tightly to the eucalyptus trees overhead and stared at the world with shiny black eyes.

My classmates scattered to different corners of the enclosure to do their projects. Huddled in my coat, I sat myself down on a bench and started sketching my favourite kangaroo – a lovely toffee-coloured one called Caramel. Kangaroos are quite easy. As long as you do them standing up with massive back legs and tiddly front ones everyone knows what you're trying to draw, unless they maybe think you're doing a wallaby.

'Nice rabbit, Taya,' commented Joe, who was scribbling the eucalyptus trees and the way their bark dangled down from the trunks and branches like silvery party-popper streamers.

'It's a *kangaroo*,' I said, stung.

'Oh, sorry,' Joe said cheerfully. He put his pencil down and tried to rub a bit of warmth back into his fingertips. 'You know, if you forget that we're freezing and squint a bit and peer through the fence like the mesh isn't there, it's like being in actual Australia, isn't it?'

I put my pencil down glumly and wondered if I could borrow the class camera. I was clearly not cut out for marsupial portraiture of the drawn variety. Glancing across the enclosure, I spotted the camera in Cash 'n' Carrie's grubby little hands. Needless to say, they were using it to take pictures of themselves instead of the animals, and squealing with laughter as they did it. Where was Ms Hutson? She was normally straight on to trouble like a homing pigeon on elastic.

As I looked around for our strangely absent teacher, my eye was caught by a flash of movement in Caramel's pouch.

'Hey,' I said, prodding Joe in excitement, 'look at that!'

'It's a kangaroo,' Joe explained. He waved his hand at the rest of the enclosure. 'There's loads of them.'

'I saw her pouch move! There must be a joey in there!' How cool would a photo of a tiny kangaroo joey be? I wondered if it would be the same colour as its mum. I had to get that camera, *right now*.

Joe laid down his pencil and squinted. 'Where?'

'There!' I said again. I packed my drawing pad away and prepared to race over and snatch the camera from Cash 'n' Carrie. I was pointing so hard, my arm was stretching like Mrs Incredible's. 'See? Again! Joe, you need glasses if you can't see that!'

It was the silence that I noticed first, followed by the sight of Tori rushing up to me at full speed. Behind her, I could see everyone standing about in uneasy clusters, drawing pads abandoned on the ground or the benches. Cash 'n' Carrie had put the class camera down and had their arms round each other.

'What's happened?' I asked, my hackles rising like a scared dog.

'Do you know where Cazza is?' Tori said, looking anxious. 'No one's seen her since Ms Hutson took her iPod. I thought she'd followed me to the viewing house where I was drawing some wombats but she didn't follow me at all. She's vanished and Ms Hutson's going *nuts*.'

I spotted Ms Hutson now, standing on the little pebbled road and talking urgently on a mobile phone, looking more frazzled than a piece of morning bacon.

'She's probably gone to the shop,' Joe offered.

Tori shook her head. 'Ms Hutson's called them. She's

called the main office too. All the keepers are on alert but no one's seen her. What if she's been kidnapped or something awful like that?'

'No way,' I said. We all knew never to accept lifts from strangers and, frankly, if someone ever tried to pull Cazza into a car they'd probably get beaten up and really, really wish they hadn't tried it in the first place. 'She'll still be in the park somewhere. You'll see.'

I wasn't feeling nearly as confident as I sounded. Cazza Turnbull made her own rules. Who knew what went on in her head half the time?

'You'll see,' I said again.

But it sounded hollow, even to me.

3

Frog on a Barbecue

Cazza wasn't in the park. She wasn't anywhere. So all we could do was pile silently back into the coach with our half-finished projects and a grim-faced Ms Hutson.

It's totally incredible the way news can travel in the blink of an eye. Judging from the hush as we entered the double doors back at school, and the round eyes that peered out of classrooms at us, the whole of Forrests had already heard about Cazza's disappearance.

We were marched back to our classroom by Mrs Digby, the Deputy Head, leaving Ms Hutson and Mr Collyer, the Head, swerving off for an urgent conference. Mrs Digby was round and sprinkled with face powder like a sugared bun. She was normally all smiles and giggles, but not today. And as for my sister, she was as tense as a tightrope preparing to take the weight of an extremely heavy elephant.

'I should have noticed something was wrong,' Tori muttered as we all bent over our books without really seeing them. 'I *knew* she was being weird today.'

'She seemed pretty normal to me,' I said, thinking about Cazza's sabre-toothed, rap-listening tiger impression.

'No, Taya. She was *weird*,' Tori insisted. 'She's been fighting loads with her mum lately and I think maybe last night's argument was some kind of final straw. I bet you she's run away.'

'Silence at the back!' shouted Mrs Digby. With her bright-yellow shirt and her short round body and her face powder clumped in cracks in her normally cheerful face, it was like being yelled at by a custard doughnut.

I don't know why I happened to glance out of the window just then, but I did. Sauntering through the school gates like she didn't have a care in the world, hands rammed hard into her black puffa jacket and shoes bouncing off the car park asphalt like an astronaut on the surface of the moon, was Cazza herself.

I nudged Tori. My twin glanced through the window and instantly rose to her feet.

'Sit!' squealed Mrs Digby.

'Please, Mrs Digby,' Tori said, and pointed. 'Cazza's back.'

'The girl did *what*?' said Dad.

Mum was so engrossed in the story that a hank of her long chocolate-brown hair was dangling unnoticed into her mug of hot coffee. Rabbit, our golden retriever, was stealthily inching towards the digestive biscuit sitting unattended on Mum's plate. Dogs have a sixth sense for when humans aren't paying attention to their food.

'Unbelievable, isn't it?' I went on, still mildly out of breath from the mad dash Tori and I had done from the bus stop to our house. 'She just strolled out of Wild World without a word to anyone, not even Tori, wandered down to Inkredible – you know, that tattoo and piercing place on Milstead Road? – and got her nose pierced with this amazing zigzag gold stud and then got back to school at more or less *exactly* the moment that her mum came squealing up in that big silver car they've got. And then Mr Collyer and Ms Hutson both zoomed out and everyone burst into this massive row in the car park. We could hear the screaming even through our classroom's double glazing.' I shook my head, lost in admiration. How had Cazza *dared*?

Tori was raiding the biscuit tin as it sat on the kitchen table between us all. It said a lot about Cazza's tale of mad rebellion that our parents — both sticklers for not scoffing any more than two biscuits at a time — totally failed to notice that she was on her third Penguin. Tori isn't very good at expressing emotions, but I can usually tell she's stressed because she eats like a Sumo wrestler. Rabbit successfully burgled Mum's digestive biscuit and took up position for Dad's.

'Please tell me that you will never do such a thing, *queridas*,' Mum begged, putting her mug down and patting Rabbit absently on her round golden head. 'Cazza's parents must have been behind themselves!'

'*Beside* themselves,' I corrected. Mum is Portuguese, so the details that make up the crazy English language sometimes catch her out.

'And in front of themselves too, I am sure!' Mum slammed the table with the palm of her hand. 'Tori, I want you to stop seeing so much of this girl. She is not the kind of person I want you to be friends with if she can do this to her teacher and to her parents!'

Tori, who was reaching for her fourth Penguin, stopped mid-stretch. 'I like her!' she said indignantly.

'The girl did a stupid thing, but Tori's too sensible to copy what her friends do,' Dad soothed, rubbing his beard between his fingers. 'As is Taya.'

I started up from a little dream I'd been having about getting my own nose stud, just like Cazza's little gold zigzag. It probably hurt like a frog on a barbecue, but would completely be worth it. 'What? Oh – yeah. I mean, no. Sure.'

'She's OK really, Mum,' Tori insisted. 'She tries to come over all hard and tough but she's like a marshmallow underneath.'

A goth marshmallow covered in skull badges, I thought.

'She's just really stressed because she's been arguing a lot with her parents lately,' Tori went on.

Thinking of parents brought me out of my nose stud dream with a thump. 'Ooh,' I said suddenly. 'Changing the subject completely here, I know, but I saw a kangaroo joey in the marsupial enclosure today!'

Tori looked surprised and I realized, what with the whole Cazza episode, I'd forgotten to tell her what I'd seen in Caramel's pouch. Mum turned her dark-chocolate eyes on me, her eyebrows lifting like two hairy drawbridges. 'Impossible,' she said.

'I did!' I beamed. 'You know that little toffee-coloured kangaroo? Caramel? When we were at the enclosure today I saw her pouch moving.'

'As I said, Taya – impossible,' said Mum. She stood up and put the mugs in the sink as Dad frowned at the nearly empty biscuit tin and tucked it back in the cupboard. Rabbit padded off to her basket with digestive crumbs around her muzzle. 'You must have imagined it. We have no kangaroo joeys at the moment.'

'How do you know?' I demanded, miffed at being dismissed straight off like this. 'Kangaroos hide their joeys for months, don't they? All tucked up safe with the milk and everything.'

'Do you mean a wallaby?' asked Tori.

'I think I know the difference between a kangaroo and a wallaby, Tori,' I said, feeling cross. Why did my family always treat me like I was an idiot? OK, so I didn't always get the best school reports, and I once thought Denmark was the capital of Sweden, but I knew my facts where animals were concerned.

Mum shook her head. 'It's impossible, as I said, Taya, because—'

'I know what I saw,' I interrupted mulishly. 'Caramel's pouch was moving the way pouches do when there are joeys inside.'

'—*because*,' Mum ploughed on, raising her voice over mine, 'we do not have any male kangaroos just now. No males, no babies. That's the way it works.'

Admittedly this was a tough one to argue and it floored me for a minute. Dad and Tori exchanged a knowing look – the one that says, 'Tut tut, Taya and that imagination of hers.'

'I definitely saw *something*,' I said in desperation. 'If it wasn't a baby joey then . . . then . . .'

'Wind?' suggested Dad.

'Kangaroos don't fart inside their pouches,' I said, unimpressed by Dad's logic. Imagine the poor little joeys if they did!

Dad rolled his eyes. 'I mean wind rippling through the fur on the kangaroo's belly, making it look as if the pouch were moving.'

I could see they weren't buying it. Well, if it was proof they needed, I'd give it to them.

Standing up from the kitchen table, I reached for my coat. 'We're all going to take a look at Caramel and prove that I'm not going mad,' I said. 'Who's coming?'

I pulled my coat on, marched to the front door and flung it open. A gust of icy wind blasted through catching hold of my scarf so that it flew up and swamped my face. Temporarily blind, I cannoned off the door frame in a distinctly uncool way.

'OK, Captain Scott of the Antarctic,' said Dad, raising his voice over Mum's and Tori's laughter as I tried to keep the look of determination on my face and ignore the way my eyes were watering with pain like a pair of bathroom taps. 'Rabbit and Tori could both use the exercise after eating all those biscuits. Let's all go and take a look at this phantom joey for ourselves.'

4

Fairies on the Compost Heap

The pain in my shoulder from the door frame incident had faded by the time we passed Sinbad the Bengal tiger and his wives in their lovely wide enclosure. They were sitting in a huddle on the rock in the middle like a huge tiger rug of cosiness. It really was cold.

'Did England just move further north?' I complained, pulling my coat more tightly around myself. My breath clouded the air. 'I'm getting icicles inside my head, like when you eat ice-cream too quickly.'

'It's called brain freeze,' said Tori, stamping her feet in a bid to warm herself up. 'Seeing how your brain's permanently frozen, I'm surprised you've noticed any difference.'

'Mum,' I complained, 'Tori's being mean!'

Mum made tutting noises at Tori, who smirked and fell silent. We all hurried up before we froze to the spot.

When we got to the marsupial enclosure, several of the animals had already started drifting off to their warm straw beds in the marsupial house, apart from the nocturnally minded ones – like the wombats and the quokkas – which were busying about and looking a lot more awake than they'd been earlier in the day. A couple of koalas were still firmly wedged in the treetops. Koalas aren't bears, by the way, even though people often call them that.

Caramel was hopping slowly around the bottom of the eucalyptus trees, sniffing out a few last remaining blades of grass before bed. Her colour was harder to see in the yellowish light of the lamp posts, but I recognized her pretty face. I pointed her out.

'There! Watch and prepare to eat your words. With extra ketchup and mustard. And hundreds and thousands.'

Sensing that we'd all stopped moving, Rabbit planted her fat bottom on the freezing-cold pebble track, then hurriedly stood up again.

'It's very cold, Taya,' Mum started, banging her arms against her sides.

Dad nodded in agreement. 'Can't we do this in the morning, love?'

My eyes were trained on Caramel like laser beams. 'We're not going anywhere until— *there*!'

A tufty something popped out of Caramel's pouch for half a blink and then popped down again. Mum gasped and put her hand to her chest.

The bitter cold was forgotten.

'I *told* you!' I crowed in triumph, and did a little celebration jig on the spot, which had the added benefit of waking up my half-dead frozen toes. 'I *told* you, didn't I? Now who's got brain freeze?'

The tufty something popped up again. It only stuck around for an extra quarter of a nanosecond but it was enough to stop me mid-jig. 'Freeze frame' has never felt like such an appropriate description.

Human eyes are incredible things. They can work things out with hardly anything to go on. Have you ever seen a word flash past your eyes for half a millisecond, maximum, and yet been able to read and understand the word like it had been sitting under your nose for hours?

Caramel was carrying a joey all right. But it was no kangaroo.

It was a koala.

* * *

To find a koala in a kangaroo pouch is unusual to say the least. Koalas stick with koalas, and kangas with kangas. Plus kangaroos can't climb trees, which is where koalas generally like to live, unless they're tree kangaroos of course, which is a whole different species Wild World doesn't have. But we'd all seen it with our own eyes and there was no denying it. Somehow Caramel the kangaroo had a little koala living in her pouch.

'I was *right* about there being a joey, even if it's not a kangaroo joey, and I want an apology for the mean stuff you said to me,' I told my sister smugly as Mum rushed off to find Sasha, the marsupial-keeper, and Dad hurried after her with Rabbit shambling along by his side. 'And you'd better make it a really good one or I might not accept it.'

'Sorr-ee,' said Tori.

I held out my hand palm-up and beckoned with my fingers, indicating that this was in no *way* apologetic enough. 'More,' I ordered.

'I am extremely totally and absolutely sorry, O Queen Taya of All Things Wild, for not believing you because you were very and completely right all along,' Tori sighed.

'Maybe you'll believe me a bit quicker next time,' I said in my most gracious voice.

Tori shrugged. 'I didn't believe you because, let's face it, your eyes aren't always very reliable.'

'If you're talking about the time I saw fairies on the compost heap, well, this is different,' I said with dignity. 'I'm no longer six years old.'

Caramel hopped lazily away from the eucalyptus trees, heading in the direction of the marsupial house. The little koala had dived out of sight again, but Tori and I could see the telltale bulge in Caramel's pouch as clear as anything.

'Do you think it's possible for kangaroos to give birth to some sort of koala–kangaroo combo?' I wondered aloud.

'Duh,' Tori said. 'Of course not. They're totally different species!'

'You can have a tiger–lion combination,' I pointed out, feeling annoyed. 'They're called ligers or tions or something like that. And horses and donkeys can give birth to mules.'

Tori looked at me pityingly. 'You need to have a bit more in common with each other than a pouch,' she said.

I didn't want this to be true but it clearly was. 'It

would be cool though, wouldn't it?' I said wistfully. 'If you could get little kangaralas. Or koalaroos.'

Mum, Dad, Rabbit and Sasha the marsupial-keeper appeared. Sasha was a tall sort of person with long dangly green-dyed hair who always reminded me of a weeping willow.

'Thanks for spotting Koko, Taya,' Sasha said. 'We noticed she wasn't with her mother about an hour ago, but we had no idea she'd moved in with Caramel.'

'Koko?' I said, enchanted. 'Is that the little koala's name?'

'That's adorable,' said Tori mistily.

'Koko was born about six months ago, but she only came out of her mother Arana's pouch last week,' Mum explained. 'She's still dependent on Arana for milk, so it is important that she returns as soon as possible.'

I gazed curiously at the koala shapes huddled up in the eucalyptus trees. 'Which one's Arana? It's a pretty name.'

'Arana means moon in one of the Aboriginal languages,' Sasha explained. 'She's the big one in the crook of the eucalyptus over there.'

I stared hard until I made out a large fluffy shape tucked into the tree Sasha was pointing at. The white tufts on Arana's ears were lit up by the yellowish lamplight behind her, making the female koala look like she was wearing a pair of glowing earmuffs. 'Was Arana worried when Koko disappeared?' I asked.

'She hasn't seemed that concerned,' Sasha admitted.

There was a bit of a kerfuffle by the marsupial house that made us all turn round. One of Sasha's assistants, a guy called Paul, had captured Caramel and was now gently lifting Koko the baby koala from the young kangaroo's pouch.

'Let's go and see the little runaway,' Sasha said with a smile. 'We'll check that she's healthy and return her to Arana tonight.'

Dad took a grateful Rabbit home to the warmth of her bed, but Mum, Tori and I weren't ready to go yet. We crowded into the marsupial house with Sasha, Paul and Koko instead.

'She's *perfect*,' I said blissfully, gazing at the ball of ash-grey fluff in Paul's big hands. I didn't want to take my eyes off Koko for a second.

'Completely and utterly perfect,' Tori agreed beside me.

Koko gave a pretty sneeze and stretched. We stared at her curved claws in fascination and her smooth black nose, which seemed way too large for her face. Paul checked her eyes and inside her mouth, made sure she wasn't too cold, and then upended her to make sure her bottom was healthy. Apparently the main problem with koalas often lies around their bottom area, so although it was probably a bit undignified for Koko we knew it was a very important thing to check.

'Come on, scrap,' said Paul at last. 'You're healthy enough. Time to go back to Mum for some dinner.'

'And on the subject of dinner . . .' Mum propelled Tori and me out of the marsupial house as Paul and Sasha disappeared back into the enclosure on their mission to reunite mother and daughter. Tori and I protested at once.

'We want to see Koko being put back with Arana!'

'I'm not hungry yet, Mum!'

'What about Caramel?'

'What about my macaroni cheese?' Mum enquired a little acidly. 'Koko and Caramel will both be fine. You can see them again tomorrow. But we will not see my macaroni cheese again tomorrow because your father and Rabbit will eat it all up.'

Reluctantly we followed Mum back home. I looked over my shoulder just before the marsupial enclosure disappeared from view. Caramel was standing beside the dimly lit eucalyptus trees, thumping her back foot on the ground. A mournful clucking noise floated towards us, like a mother hen calling her chick back home.

5

Great White Shark with Grey Bits

'It's so weird,' I said as we gazed through the fence of the marsupial enclosure the following morning.

Everything sparkled with frost in the early light, as if a winter fairy had swept her wand around and sprinkled the world with magic. If anything, it was even colder than the day before and my feet were already hurting from the chill even though we'd only left the house five minutes earlier. We had diverted from our normal route through the park to catch the bus so we could check up on Koko and the other marsupials.

'I mean,' I went on, 'has Caramel officially adopted Koko or something?'

Caramel the kangaroo was hopping around the frosty grass with two fluffy koala ears peeping out of her pouch. The evidence was unmistakable. Despite Paul and Sasha's best efforts last night, Koko had already moved back in.

'Looks like it,' said Tori.

'But it's *weird*,' I repeated. 'Don't you think?'

'Mum's always adopting animals that are different species from us,' Tori pointed out. 'There's no reason why animals shouldn't do it as well.' She glanced up into the trees. 'And Arana looks like she couldn't care less.'

Arana had barely moved from where she'd been sitting the day before. All I could see were her jaws moving up and down as she munched on her eucalyptus-leaf breakfast. Koalas basically eat nothing but eucalyptus leaves. They never even have a drink of water because they get all their moisture from the leaves. Dull or what? Imagine your whole life laid out in front of you as a bunch of plates covered in steamed broccoli. Though maybe koalas actually look forward to their eucalyptus the way we look forward to a doughnut, and a life full of end-to-end doughnuts maybe wouldn't be so bad.

'Caramel seems really happy,' I said, staring at the long-legged kangaroo. 'Her lips are curled into a sort of smile. Don't you think?'

Tori rolled her eyes at me. She never appreciates my leaps of fantasy.

A strange growling noise made us both jump.

'That sounded like a lion,' I said in astonishment.

'Wild World doesn't have lions,' Tori replied with a frown.

'I know!'

The growling started again. It made my hair stand on end. Startled, we hunted for the source. What was it? Had there been a breakout from one of the big cat enclosures? And more's the point: was the escapee hungry?

Our eyes settled back on the marsupial enclosure.

'I think it was a koala,' I said slowly.

Tori scoffed. 'Don't be—'

The biggest koala in the nearest tree curled its furry lip and growled again. Tori trailed away into silence.

'It *was* the koala!' I gasped. 'That is the craziest noise I've ever heard!'

A noise answered from a tree a bit further away. I picked out a second koala, its fur darker but fluffier than the first growler. Arana chewed in a bored sort of way, roughly halfway between the two.

'I think they're staking their claims to Arana's attention,' Tori said.

'You mean, they're growling because they fancy her?' I asked, just to be clear.

Tori nodded.

Unbelievable! Koalas, the cutest furballs *ever*, snarling at each other like a couple of tiny lions! It should have been funny but somehow it wasn't.

'Our bus!' Tori said suddenly.

We legged it towards the gates. Behind us, we heard the two boy koalas growling at each other again. I had a flash memory of cuddly Koko's long, curved black claws. Who'd have thought it? It was like discovering your favourite teddy had just sprouted fangs.

And on the subject of fangs . . .

'Don't talk to her,' Tori cautioned as we waited to go into assembly. 'In fact, I recommend you don't even look her in the eye if you want your head still attached to your neck in Science.'

Pacing up and down in front of us, rhythmically banging her fists on the opposite walls of the corridor and aiming kicks at the fire extinguisher each time she passed it, Cazza was doing a fine impression of a famished puma preparing to rip the throat out of the first wild pig foolish enough to cross her path.

'I'm not looking, OK?' I muttered back nervously.

But of course, when your brain is screaming at your eyes *not* to do something, what do your eyes go and do?

'What?' Cazza had caught my sudden involuntary blink spasm in her direction. 'What are you staring at, loser?'

'Nothing!' I stammered helplessly.

'Staring at my *nose* are you, loser?' Cazza hissed, advancing towards me. 'Staring at the sad little hole where my sad loser not-parents made me take my piercing out? Are you? *Are you?*'

My eyes helplessly flashed to the little hole, red and sore-looking, and mourned the loss of that fantastic little golden zigzag that had caused so much trouble yesterday. I flattened myself against the wall as the rest of 7H looked at me with a combination of sympathy and relief that it wasn't them in the firing line.

'Calm down, Caz,' Tori began.

'YOU ARE!' Cazza howled, ignoring my sister and still bearing down on me. 'YOU—'

Ms Hutson loomed up like a great white shark with grey bits. Her voice was low but deadly.

'Mr Collyer's office, Catherine. *Now.*'

Very deliberately, Cazza aimed a massive kick at the top of the fire extinguisher. The trigger bit, already pretty battered, flew off with a bang – and coated the corridor and most of 7H with stinking foam. There were shrieks of shock and disgust as everyone tried to leap backwards, away from the mad thrashing tube shooting white stuff everywhere. Practically everyone got hit. It was like one of those Saturday morning shows except no one was laughing.

Even I could see that Cazza had gone too far this time. In fact, I could hardly believe how unbelievably uncool the coolest girl in Year Seven had just been.

'Cazza Turnbull is a total *nutcase*,' I spluttered as our eyeball-poppingly furious teacher marched Cazza down the corridor, shouting for someone to come and sort out the mess. 'Tori, why are you friends with her? She's a rabid wolf!'

Mrs Digby and the school caretaker came hurrying towards us, Mrs Digby waving for calm and being more or less completely ignored. There was a dangerous smell of recklessness and overexcitement and fire-extinguishing chemicals in the air, and Mrs Digby was in no way equipped to deal with it. To be perfectly honest, the only way she'd have got 7H's attention just then was if she'd been wearing riot gear and a helmet.

Tori wiped a bit of foam off the sleeve of her jumper. 'She needs friends,' was all she said.

'She needs a *cage*!' I was still trembling. 'Why does she act so unbelievably crazy all the time? And don't say it's because she's been fighting with her mum. We fight with *our* mum, but we don't cause World War Three in the school corridors!'

Tori flicked the last bit of foam off her skirt. 'Her mum's not her real mum,' she said reluctantly. 'Cazza's adopted.'

6

Blimey Jam with Blueberries

'Why have I never known this about Cazza? Why have you never told me?'

I'd been asking Tori this for most of the day. But every time I tried to get an answer she'd hissed at me to stop talking about it. Now it was nearly four o'clock and we were back at Wild World and my sister *still* hadn't answered my question.

'Why can't you just drop it?' Tori said in desperation.

'Aren't I trustworthy enough? Too stupid to understand? What? Tell me!'

When I'm in PBM – Persistent Badger Mode – I've noticed how results usually follow the first sign of despair from my opponent. Like, I know Dad's close to giving in to whatever I'm PBMing about when he does this helpless snort that sounds like a firework in a shoebox, and I always turn the pressure up ever so slightly straight after the snort and get my answer/chocolate bar/pair of shoes shortly afterwards (OK, maybe not the shoes, but there's a first time for everything). Tori was proving a harder nut to crack than Dad, but she finally caved as we reached the chimp enclosure.

'I promised Caz I'd never talk about her being adopted with anyone, OK?' she said wearily. 'There, now I've broken my promise *again* so does that make you feel better?'

Finally we were getting somewhere. 'But why the big secret?' I asked. 'Lots of people are adopted.'

Tori heaved a great swell of a sigh.

'She's only just found out,' I said, suddenly understanding. 'Hasn't she?'

Tori rested her hands on the mesh surrounding the chimps, who were gambolling and playing like hairy nutters on the frozen ground and assorted climbing platforms in their enclosure – most likely to warm themselves up.

'She found out a week before she started at Forrests. I only discovered it because I overheard her yelling something at her mum when I was round at hers last week. She denied it when I asked about it at first. But then everything suddenly burst out of her like . . . like . . .'

'Like squeezing a massive spot?' I suggested helpfully. 'Pus and everything?'

Tori winced. 'Thanks for the gross image. I had to promise on my life not to tell anyone, not even you.' She looked at her feet, the picture of gloom. 'Bang bang, guess I'm dead.'

'I'm your sister; I don't count,' I said. 'Anyway, everyone says twins can read each other's minds so you didn't actually have to tell me out loud because I already knew on this well deep spiritual level. Do you think maybe she's never talked to anyone about it until you?'

Tori lifted her shoulders. 'I guess she must have talked about it with her parents when she found her adoption papers.'

The significance of the word 'found' clonked me round the head like a large boxing glove. 'Her parents didn't actually *tell* her?' I asked incredulously. 'She found out by *accident*?'

How must that have felt? Growing up with people you thought were your parents, only to discover – with no warning – that they were basically strangers with no blood connection to you at all? The nose people thought you'd inherited from your dad, the colour of your hair that all your mates said was the same as your mum's – all of it coincidence and none of it true.

'Blimey jam with blueberries,' I said with feeling.

Back at home, a strange white box with wires and buttons on the kitchen top caught our attention and put Cazza's problems to one side.

'An incubator!' I dropped my school bag on the hall floor and rushed up to the box at top speed. Incubators meant baby creatures and, as everyone who knows me could tell you, baby creatures are my complete and utter favourite thing. 'Mum! What have we got?'

Mum zoomed out of the airing cupboard with her arms full of stuff, her long dark hair tangled up on top of her head in a shiny chocolate nest. 'No time to talk, *queridas*,' she panted. 'Power cut in part of the tropical house, only just discovered – it is all hands in the deck today to save what we can.'

Tori and I both gasped. If you're a tropical animal in Surrey in February when the temperature's below freezing and your heating goes off . . .

'What did we lose?' Tori's braver than me at asking questions like that.

'Some birds and reptiles.' Mum's jaw trembled and she clamped it shut. She adores all animals, but her favourites have always been the reptiles.

The phone started ringing in that insistent way that always seems to go with crises in our house. Mum shoved the armful of towels and sheets into Tori's arms with instructions to find somewhere to put them, and rushed for the phone.

'Plug the incubator in the airing cupboard!' she called as she reached for the receiver. 'I have made space. We need all the warmth we can get – if it's not too late already.'

Tori started towards the incubator, hardly able to see over the top of her towel mountain. I stopped her.

'I think those' – I prodded the towels and made them wobble – 'are going to make picking up an incubator a little tricky. I'll deal with this.'

Tori rushed up the stairs with the towels as I hefted the incubator up in my arms, trying to peer through the milky lid and work out what I was carrying. It was very light and there was no sense of movement inside. I put it on the empty shelf in the airing cupboard and plugged it in.

Mum hung up and dashed back towards the kitchen, tripping over the school bag I'd left lying in the hall.

'How many times do I tell you to put your bag away when you come home, Taya?' she shouted.

'Sorry,' I said hurriedly. I glanced back at the incubator with its little light burning steadily at me on the airing-cupboard shelf. 'So, Mum, what—'

AND the phone was off again. Mum shot back to the hall, tripping over Rabbit's tail this time. Rabbit yelped, plunged into the kitchen and crashed into the bin as her feet slid sideways on a towel that Tori had managed to drop. The noise was enough to blow your head off.

'Peace and tranquillity as usual, I see,' Dad remarked as he let himself in the kitchen door.

I told him what was going on to the best of my ability, stroking Rabbit's head to assure her she hadn't looked too stupid. Dad looked grave.

'Is your mum in charge of resuscitating anything?'

I nodded at the white box on the airing-cupboard shelf. 'That,' I said.

'Do we know what it is?'

'Mum's too busy to ask. And I don't want to open the lid in case I end up harming whatever's inside.'

Dad regarded the little box. 'Well, I'm guessing it's not an elephant,' he said.

I peered more closely at the semi-opaque lid. Now

that the incubator was on, light was sort of glowing through it – and what looked like two little white balls were nestling inside. A little light of my own went on in my brain.

'Eggs!' I gasped.

Eggs meant chicks, and chicks meant fluffballs – and *tropical* eggs probably meant multicoloured fluffballs, which are the best sort of fluffballs there are.

Now all we had to do was wait and see if they had survived.

7

Please, Please, Please, Dear Egg God

'It exploded?' Joe repeated disbelievingly.

'There were bits of fried rat everywhere,' I said with relish. 'The stupid creature nibbled through a major electricity cable – the kind which would kill a full-grown person, let alone a titchy rodent. That's why the power went out. They've had all the reptile and small mammal-keepers working flat out to save as many animals as they can. Fingers – he's one of the reptile-keepers – has got twelve half-frozen lizards on twenty-four-hour watch. I think the rat's tail ended up somewhere on the tropical-house roof. A bird will have eaten it by now, thinking it was just a bony worm.'

'Can we stop talking about this?' Tori begged, looking grossed out.

I wouldn't normally have enjoyed talking about an exploded rat, but you have to understand that this one's dumb little ratty appetite had killed four defenceless birds and two quite rare lizards, probably several of the little creatures being watched right now by their worried keepers, and maybe our incubator eggs too. So I think I'm allowed a bit of gory storytelling.

'Stopping now,' I said reluctantly. 'So we're all just waiting to see whether the eggs survived or whether the chicks inside got too cold. We'll know in a day or two.'

'I wish I could hatch tropical birds in our airing cupboard,' said Joe. 'Maybe I'll ask Dad if we could try it.'

I pictured Joe's airing cupboard, which was most likely full of his dad's work socks and neatly ironed shirts. Somehow I couldn't see Mr Morton going for the egg-hatching idea.

'Any word from Cazza?' Joe asked next.

'She called me last night.' Tori looked relieved at the change of subject. 'She's really upset about being suspended. She says her parents are hardly speaking to her but that she doesn't care, which of course means exactly the opposite.'

'Well, she shouldn't have kicked off the way she did,' Heather Cashman butted in in her moaniest voice. 'That foam stuff totally ruined my shoes. She needs to go to a mental hospital.'

'Yeah,' added Carrie Taylor on cue.

'Who asked you to join our conversation?' Tori demanded, rising to Cazza's defence. 'Our friend's having a hard time right now, OK?'

'And we really don't give a frog's fart for your shoes, Heather,' I added.

Heather retreated, spluttering something about Tori and her Tordis – a joke which had grown dull about three seconds after Carrie'd come up with it. Tori picked up where she'd left off.

'Cazza says she might come back on Monday on a behavioural deal she's made with Mr Collyer. She'll sign this bit of paper saying she won't misbehave any more and the school will let her stay.'

I raised my eyebrows. A bit of paper? Wasn't that like trying to block a raging river with one of those holey bags you buy oranges in? I did feel really sorry for Cazza about the way she'd found out about being adopted – but how could anyone imagine signing a bit of paper would fix things?

'She says she's prepared to sign it,' Tori went on. 'So

I guess she's going to try a bit harder to . . .'

'Be normal?' I suggested.

Tori shrugged a bit helplessly. 'I guess.'

An image of the electricity cable and the rat crept back into my head. The odds had never been in the rat's favour, because the electricity cable had been a lot bigger and more dangerous. It wasn't a huge leap, even to a dozy brain like mine, to compare Mr Collyer's bit of paper to that unfortunate rodent.

We were home and enjoying the peace of Friday night when Mum yelled at us from the kitchen.

'Come quick! Something is happening!'

Rabbit practically took off with fright as Tori and I pelted out of the sitting room and screeched over to the airing cupboard, where Mum and Dad were both peering at the incubator with excitement. Mum had opened the little box a fraction, just enough so we could see one of the eggs was moving. It was slight but unmistakable – just like the way I'd first spotted Koko in Caramel's pouch.

'That's brilliant!' I squealed. It meant at least one of the chicks had survived!

'They look like chicken eggs,' said Tori, peering more closely. 'What kind of birds are they going to be?'

I caught Mum exchanging winks with Dad. They're always winking at each other or snogging these days.

'Let's just wait and see,' said Dad. He loves spinning stuff out like this.

'So now what?' asked Tori.

'More waiting,' Mum said. 'But at least we know we are waiting for a guaranteed event! Call for a takeaway, Andy *querido*. I want to celebrate.'

The incubator lid was carefully lowered again, and we left the eggs to their own devices as we quarrelled happily over whether to have rice or noodles, or rice *and* noodles, from our fave Chinese takeaway.

'I will keep watch all night tonight,' Mum announced. 'These eggs are very precious and I will have *no* problems when they are in my house.'

She said this so fiercely that I imagined any problems lurking outside the back door muttering to each other in a depressed sort of way, 'No point going in there, mate, not with this one in charge.'

'Can we help?' asked Tori.

'Yay!' I said, gleefully imagining some serious late-night telly.

'Go on, Neet,' said Dad, squeezing Mum round the middle. 'It's the weekend and the girls are keen.'

After a bit of squabbling, Tori said she'd do the first

few hours and Mum went for the bit in the middle of the night, leaving me with what radio presenters call the graveyard shift of four o'clock in the morning. Dad has got diabetes, and getting up in the middle of the night would mess about with his insulin and his blood sugar, so it wasn't a good idea for him to help.

'I will wake you if there is any news,' Mum soothed, pushing him up the stairs like a reluctant sheep after our takeaway.

'Bad luck, Dad,' I called after him, settling down in one of our armchairs and reaching for the TV remote.

Mum pointed at me. 'Go to bed now as well, Taya.'

I gawped. 'But it's only nine o'clock!'

'You will thank me when you must get up at four o'clock tomorrow morning. Go!' Mum ordered.

I was actually pretty tired because we'd had a busy week, but I glared at Mum for the sake of it. Tori took the remote like it belonged to her and flicked to Channel Geek, which was showing something about meteorites.

'Enjoy your show about rocks,' I said sarcastically.

'I will, thanks,' Tori answered.

Please, please, please, dear Egg God, I thought as I mounted the stairs. Don't let them hatch until at least four o'clock tomorrow morning.

* * *

I was sitting bolt upright the moment Mum touched my shoulder in the darkness. Tori was snoring peacefully on the other side of the room.

'Did they hatch?'

Mum put her hand to her yawny mouth and shook her head at the same time. 'But we have some movement in the second egg too,' she told me quietly. 'Downstairs now – dressing gown, slippers. OK?'

As Mum dragged herself to bed, I scooted down the stairs with delight, giving the Egg God the thumbs-up. Rabbit was cross-eyed with exhaustion, being entirely unused to people moving around the kitchen finding biscuits – I mean, toast . . . OK, I do mean biscuits – in the middle of the night. It was all she could do to wag her tail at me before her big head flumped back down in her basket. I peeped into the incubator. The first egg was rocking quite hard, but there were no cracks yet. The second one gave a little heave and then went quiet again. Deciding to check them every ten minutes, I went into the sitting room and turned the TV on in happy anticipation of a telly-fest of early-morning joy.

I endured twenty minutes of a shopping channel, a horrible American show about enormously fat people, and the news, before I turned it off again. Talk about *disappointment*.

At 4.31 I wandered back to the airing cupboard for another look. Neither egg was moving now. How long was this going to take?

I think I actually twiddled my thumbs at this point. The moon outside was huge and white as ice, and even the animals in the park outside the kitchen window were in silent mode. I went for another biscuit. Rabbit was already ignoring me and snoring by the cooker again. I paced up and down for at *least* ten years, but when I finally allowed myself to look at the clock again, it only said 4.53.

'Oh, no *way*!'

My voice sounded big and spooky, and I found myself getting a wee bit freaked out. This awake-at-night business was no fun at all.

I curled up in the squishiness of the sofa again, prepared out of sheer desperation to give the fat TV Americans another go. Almost instantly, I yawned. My eyelids were so *heavy*, like they were lined with stones . . .

I heaved them open in a panic and discovered that the fat people weren't on the TV any more. I gazed at the clock with gummy eyes. Did it say 5.27? If the eggs had hatched and I'd missed it, Mum'd kill me!

I returned to the airing cupboard at speed. Lifting the lid, I almost dropped it again with a squeal. I was seeing things. Or was I still asleep?

The contents of the incubator made no sense at all. Because instead of two small white eggs, or even a pair of newly hatched birds, I found myself looking at a tiny-weeny . . .

Crocodile.

8

Titanium-Toothed Alien

I shut the lid quickly and concentrated on the surprisingly difficult art of breathing for a second or two. I was asleep for sure. How could I wake myself up?

I pinched myself hard, as that's what people do in books and on films.

'OW!'

So I *was* awake! I lifted the incubator lid again with trembling fingers.

The crocodile – cayman? alligator? – inside was about twelve centimetres long, with a shiny tail and beautiful markings all down its body. It gazed up at me from the remains of its egg with huge, glowing green eyes, and made this funny squeaky-toy noise. It was completely perfect, except for a little bit of shell sitting on its head like a rather stupid hat.

'Oh my wombats,' I whispered, gripping tightly to the box lid. 'MUUUUUM!'

Rabbit rocketed out of bed like a hairy explosion, barking her head off at my shout. There was a bang and a thump, then Mum came racing down the stairs with her hair tangled into big lumps and her PJ bottoms falling down. 'What? What? It has hatched?'

'It's a crocodile! Or a cayman! Or an alli-wotsit!'

Mum put her hands to her face in ecstasy. She started crooning at the little beast in Portuguese, and it squeaked again and snapped its perfect tiny jaws at her, making its eggshell hat fall off.

'You didn't *tell* me!' I said plaintively.

'Did you enjoy the surprise?' Laughing, Mum stroked the little creature. It squeaked again and tried to bite her thumb. 'Oh! I must call Fingers right away and tell him we have one beautiful Nile crocodile safely hatched! Keep watching for the second one, OK?'

As Mum dashed for the phone, Tori appeared in the hall, followed by Dad. Dad didn't seem that surprised to find the little croc gazing up at him but Tori nearly leaped out of her *Doctor Who* dressing gown.

'So much for tropical birds!' she gasped. 'You knew,

didn't you, Dad? That's why you and Mum were winking at each other last night!'

'I suppose I did know,' Dad said seriously. 'I was just in de-Nile.'

'It's a Nile crocodile, Tor,' I said, giggling at the bewilderment on my sister's face. 'Are you still asleep or what? It's usually you explaining Dad's jokes to *me*.'

Mum was yakking on the phone at a hundred miles an hour and Rabbit was going totally nuts at all the excitement, bum-skidding around the hall like her tail had an outboard motor attached to it. And me? Well. *There was a Nile crocodile in my airing cupboard!* Now that I was coming down off the ceiling, I gazed at the tiny shiny beast before me and realized that I was in love. Crocodiles aren't traditionally the cuddliest or cutest of animals but, believe me, if you'd been where I was right then, you would have fallen in love too.

The little creature was still staring steadily at me, its eyes clear and green and as beautiful as a light-filled garden pond. Its enquiring little squeak wrapped my head in pink tissue paper and smothered my brain in little pink bows. I started feeling a bit tearful.

'Wild World doesn't have Nile crocodiles,' said Tori, practical as ever. 'How come we've got these eggs?'

There was a rat-a-tat on the front door. Mum opened it and a stocky little guy with close-cropped black hair came stumping out of the darkness into the house, his tired face ablaze with excitement.

'Good news at last!' he said in a cheerful Irish accent. 'Believe me, I could do with some after the night I've had. Where's our newest member of the Wild World family then?'

Fingal O'Connor was known as Fingers to everyone at Wild World, and most probably to everyone else in his life as well, because he had only two fingers on one hand. With a job handling some of Wild World's most dangerous animals – caymans and alligators and other assorted reptiles – it was quite surprising that all of his other limbs were still attached to his body. Tori and I spent hours playing 'How Fingers Lost His Fingers', building up mad storylines to fit the facts. My personal favourite was one we'd come up with a few weeks ago, about how he'd heroically pulled a baby from the dripping jaws of a titanium-toothed alien (that was Tori's bit) and returned it to the hysterically grateful Queen of Greenland, who'd made him a prince and ordered a pair of golden fingers with diamond fingernails to replace the ones he'd lost, which had then tragically got swept away to sea when a tidal wave demolished the whole of the Queen of Greenland's palace and (Tori's bit again) the titanium-toothed alien's fleet of warp-speed battle cruisers at the same time. Everything about Fingers was heroic, from the gleam in his bright blue eyes to the huge white smile he flashed at everyone, cold- and warm-blooded alike.

'Well, aren't you gorgeous!' he exclaimed on catching sight of the baby croc. He picked it up and studied it in the overhead light. The tiddler squeaked at him and buried its tiny pinlike fangs into his little finger. 'A boy!' he declared, apparently unbothered by the dozen little crocodile teeth embedded in his knuckle despite the fact that he really couldn't afford to lose another finger. 'And a feisty one too!'

'I was the first person to see him,' I said proudly.

The other egg started rocking violently as if in response to all the voices. Fingers put the baby down and picked up the egg instead. 'Come on, you little darling, let's give you a hand,' he said, rolling the egg between his palms. If it had been me inside that shell, I think I'd have started feeling sick the way you do when you're rolling down a hill.

'The mum and dad would normally roll the egg in their mouths to crack it a little,' he added for our benefit, 'and allow the little one to climb out easier. My mouth's not big enough, but my hands should do the trick.'

Within moments a second croc had unfurled from the eggshell in Fingers's hands and started wrapping its tail around his wrist. This one was paler and smaller than the first, with more of a mud-brown head than its brother. A girl.

Fingers set the girl back down in the incubator with her brother. The crocs faced each other with their little jaws wide open. It was probably meant to look threatening, but I thought it was more like they were smiling at each other.

'One of each!' said Mum happily. 'We will have this whole park full of crocodiles very soon.'

This was a slightly scary thought, but cool at the same time. The Wild World Croc Experience! Maybe Matt, the manager, would go for the idea big time, and we'd have log flumes and glass-bottomed boats and feeding time and—

'Any breeding programme is some way off,' said Fingers. 'Nile crocs nearly became extinct you know, about fifty years ago but they're thriving again today. Amazing creatures. We've wanted to study them for years here at Wild World. And now, thanks to the conservation project we've been working with in Kenya that sent us these two eggs, we can!'

He rummaged in his bag and produced a Tupperware box from the depths.

'What's in there?' I asked curiously. The way things were going, I wouldn't have been surprised if the box contained a snake.

'Grub,' Fingers answered cheerfully, prising open the box and setting it down on the side. 'We need to feed these babies right away.'

Croc number one crashed his gnashers together to remind everyone present that he was already more than capable of dismembering a cow, provided the cow had been miniaturized in advance. He still hadn't taken his eyes off me.

I did the next bit without thinking. Reaching into the box for a bit of food, I tossed it to him. 'Here you go, tiddler!'

'Whoa!' said Fingers sharply.

But it was too late. The little crocodile had already gobbled up his first meal. He turned his green headlamps and stared at me again, even more intently than before. It was a bit unnerving, actually.

'What?' I said, feeling defensive at the silence that had suddenly descended. 'You said to feed them right away!'

'I did,' Fingers admitted. He threw a bit of food at the girl crocodile, who chomped it up nearly as quickly as her brother. 'Only I kind of thought – I would be the one to do the feeding.'

'Has Taya done something wrong?' Tori asked.

'Not wrong,' said Fingers. He put the lid back on the food and scratched his head. 'Just . . . complicated.'

I squirmed. The little crocodile had been so cute and he'd been looking at me so hungrily . . . I hoped I hadn't harmed him in some way.

'Well,' Fingers said at last, 'there's nothing for it but to tell you the happy news. Taya? Welcome to motherhood.'

I looked from Fingers back to the baby crocodile, whose eyes were still trained on me like a tiny pair of green searchlights. My throat felt oddly dry.

'But I'm not his mother,' I said.

Fingers's eyes twinkled at me. 'You are now.'

9

Green in a Certain Light

'It's called imprinting,' Fingers explained. 'Newly hatched crocs will often focus on the first creature they see and form a bond, particularly if that creature feeds it. Traditionally it's the croc parents. As these little tiddlers don't have a mum or a dad – they were both killed by hunters back in Kenya – I was planning to play mother. But I didn't feed the little male. You did. Plus, you were the first living thing he saw when he came out of the egg.'

'But I don't look anything like a crocodile!' I protested.

'Oh, I don't know,' said Tori, leaning back against the airing-cupboard door. 'I've always thought your teeth were quite pointy.'

'And your skin looks green in a certain light,' Dad added.

'Oh, thanks a million!' I said crossly as everyone burst out laughing.

'Stroke his head,' suggested Fingers. 'He'll let you, you know.'

I nervously pictured the way the little crocodile had tried to bite Mum and then sunk his teeth into Fingers without any hesitation. 'He'll bite me! I mean, he's really cute and everything, but I actually quite like my fingers and I need them, thanks very much!' And I couldn't help flashing a glance at Fingers's funny-looking hand.

The baby crocodile lifted one yellow foot, like he was waving at me, and gave another of his funny little squeaks.

'Aah,' said Mum fondly, like we were all looking at a weeny fluffy kitten.

'I think he's saying: "Mama, your teeth are pathetic",' Tori said, weak with laughter.

'And so's your nose,' Dad put in, which made my twin lose it all over again.

'What is this, Bash Taya Day?' I demanded, raising my voice over the racket. 'I'll stroke him and then we'll see who's laughing, OK? There!'

I shot my hand into the incubator and stroked the little crocodile on the head. He actually closed his eyes like he was enjoying the attention. Unlike with Mum and Fingers, he didn't twist his head and try and take a chunk out of me. With dawning wonder, I realized Fingers was right. I stroked him again, more boldly this time. Taking my hand back in some triumph, I challenged my guffawing sister.

'Your turn now.'

'Me?' Tori stopped mid-laugh. 'No way!'

I stroked my scaly new son meaningfully. 'Laugh one more time and I'll put my crocodile in your bed one night extremely soon.'

'So what are you going to call him, Taya *querida*?' asked Mum, laughing at the genuinely worried look on Tori's face.

'Easy,' I said, feeling a bit more gracious. '2thi like the rapper, because he is. But I will spell it T-O-O-T-H-Y just to make Tori happy, not that she deserves it.'

Tori smiled at me in surprise, saying sorry and thanks all in one go.

'Do you want to name the girl, Tori?' asked Fingers.

'Ooh, yes!' said my sister enthusiastically. 'How about Sarah-Jane?'

There is seriously no hope on this earth that my

twin will *ever* learn to be cool.

'I had planned to take these crocs back to the tropical house with me as soon as they hatched,' Fingers said. He scratched his head again. 'Only something tells me that young Toothy is going to have a problem with that.'

Toothy opened his bright-yellow jaws and did another one of his foot waves.

'You mean, we can keep him?' I asked in delight. Seriously, how many eleven-year-olds get to have a crocodile as a pet?

'We'll wean him off you slowly, so you won't have him for ever,' Fingers said. 'But if it's OK with you, Anita, I think it would be best to leave him here for now. I'll take Sarah-Jane, settle her in at the tropical house. Toothy can join her in a week or two.'

'So the power in the tropical house has been reconnected?' Tori asked.

'We've had an engineer on it half the night and all is toasty and warm again. The animals are being rehoused this morning, though I'm sorry to say we lost two more lizards and a clutch of finch eggs overnight despite our best efforts.'

I wasn't taking in much of what Fingers was saying because I was feeling dazed all over again. OK, we weren't exactly *keeping* Toothy, but we would have him for at least a week! There was loads of stuff I could do with him for a week. I imagined taking him out for a little walk on a tiny little crocodile lead. I might even be allowed to take him into school to show everyone! My cool factor would be off the iceberg scale!

'I'll clear my timetable with Matt,' Mum was saying to Fingers. 'I have special status when young animals need extra attention; there will be no problem.'

'That's settled then,' Fingers agreed. 'Do you have a tank you can keep Toothy in for now, Anita?'

Mum dashed off to the cupboard by the back door which was stuffed with animal-fostering kit like feeding bottles, teats, droppers, antiseptic dressings, flea treatments, boxes, lids – and a small fish tank saved from a refurb of the aquarium in the tropical house. 'What about this?'

'Trust your mum to have all the right stuff to hand,' Fingers said, winking at me. 'I'll fetch more food later on for you. Keep him warm in the airing cupboard for now – I'll get you a heat lamp as soon as I can.'

I got busy helping Mum clean out the fish tank, which was a bit dusty but otherwise perfect for Toothy's temporary new home. Mum found a bottle of distilled water to pour in the bottom while I dashed outside into the bitter chill of the morning to find a nice flat stone for Toothy to sit on when he wasn't swimming about. Baby crocodiles can swim as soon as they are born, lucky things.

We boiled the stone to sterilize it and warmed up the water a bit. Then we put everything in the fish tank together and slid it on to the airing-cupboard shelf beside the incubator.

Fingers nodded at me. 'Over to you, Mum.'

'Come on, Toothykins,' I said in my softest and most motherly voice.

Tori laughed but then stopped, most likely remembering my little promise about tucking Toothy under her duvet. Very carefully I scooped up my crocodile from the incubator box. He sat quietly in my hand as I lifted him over the lip of the fish tank and put him on the flat rock. Then he did a little foot wave and clacked his teeth together a couple of times before sliding quickly off the stone and into the water, so that he was totally submerged apart from his emerald-coloured eyes.

'Easy as pie,' said Fingers.

I rested my chin on the airing-cupboard shelf and stared lovingly through the glass at Toothy as he swam about, exploring his new home. It was incredible to think he'd been out of his egg for little more than an hour.

My crocodile – for now at least. I planned to enjoy every second of his stay.

10

Mummy Cloud

"Can you pull your head out of your mummy cloud, please, Taya?'

I jerked out of a daydream where I was holding Toothy under my arm in the school canteen and all the scary kids in the upper years were standing on the tables and making girly screaming noises. 'Of course!' I said generously. 'What's up?'

'For the second time,' said Tori in a patient voice, 'Fingers wants to take Sarah-Jane back to the tropical house and I thought I'd go too. D'you want to come?'

Toothy was watching us all through the glass wall of his tank. He wouldn't need feeding again for a little while, but he might miss me if I went out of his sight. Then again, I did really want to see the new bit that

Fingers had organized for the baby crocs in the tropical house. I bit my lip and watched Fingers wrapping Sarah-Jane and her incubator up in a thick woolly blanket, preparing for the cold outside. I'd only been a mother for about half an hour and problems were already starting to peep over the windowsill of my life and wave their knobbly little arms for my attention. How did mothers with human babies cope?

'He will be fine,' Mum said, seeing my torn expression. 'He's not hungry and he's happy in his new tank.'

'Besides,' Fingers put in, 'he'll have to get used to seeing less of his mother next week when you're at school, right?'

Talk about opportunity! I swung round to Mum eagerly. 'Perhaps I shouldn't actually go to school next week! Toothy's welfare is more important than Maths and English and stuff. He's only just been born. Making me leave him would be completely cruel and unnecessary!'

'Fingers and I will play mother while you are learning all those useful lessons for your future,' said Mum, unimpressed by my argument.

'Go,' Dad ordered from the cooker where he was breaking eggs into a saucepan. 'But make sure you're back in half an hour or all the scrambled eggs will be gone. Don't say you weren't warned.'

I grabbed my coat and followed Tori, Fingers and the well-wrapped-up incubator out into the chilly morning. For a moment it looked like Rabbit would follow us – but she was so knackered from the night's excitements that she made it about three steps towards the door before she collapsed in a large yellow heap on the kitchen floor again.

It was still barely seven o'clock in the morning and the sun was just starting to peer through the bare branches of the trees in the zebra paddocks. Our breath mushroomed into the air, making parachutes of whiteness all around us. Fingers tucked the incubator closer to his chest as we walked, whispering sweet nothings to Sarah-Jane. It was pretty hilarious for a big guy with bristle-cut hair and a bunch of missing fingers. He was clearly nuts about his new baby.

In the marsupial enclosure, Koko's mum Arana was still up the same tree she'd been in on Friday morning. The two males crouched motionless in the trees on either side.

'I don't think those koalas ever move,' Tori said.

'If you had your breakfast, lunch and supper within reach all day long, would you?' I reasoned.

I looked for Koko. Once again, the bulge in a contented-looking Caramel's pouch told its own story.

'Funny, isn't it?' I said. We jogged to catch up with Fingers and Sarah-Jane as they disappeared into the tropical house next door. 'Everyone's adopting different species at the moment. Caramel and Koko. Me and Toothy. The Turnbulls and Cazza.'

'She's not a different species,' said Tori.

This was a minor detail in my opinion. 'You know what I mean.'

'I hope Caz is OK,' Tori said glumly. 'I haven't heard from her since she called on Thursday night. Her folks have probably confiscated her phone again.'

The blast of heat in the tropical house was *gorgeous*. I think I actually sighed with joy as we came through the doors and into the steamy warmth. Lizards and snakes blinked at us from their tanks, the heaters humming over our heads like furious bees.

An area for the baby crocs had been set aside towards the back of the house, up at around waist-height to make access easier for the keepers. There was an expanse of yellow sand and several flat rocks, plus a swimming pool for Sarah-Jane – and eventually Toothy – to swim in. A heat lamp burned merrily overhead.

'Look at that water!' said Fingers. 'Doesn't it make you want to dive in?'

As he set the little crocodile down on the clean warm sand, Sarah-Jane opened her mouth and crouched motionless for a few seconds. Then she did this sinewy little gallop and plunged into the water.

'It's like a holiday camp for crocodiles,' I said. When Toothy moved in, he was going to love it!

'All that's missing is the entertainment,' said Tori with one of her famous straight faces.

'What will you do when they get too big for this tank, Fingers?' I knew that fully grown Nile crocodiles could grow up to six metres long.

Fingers tapped his nose. 'Plans are afoot. Wild World will become Reptile Central before you know it.'

Reptile Central sounded encouragingly like my idea for the Wild World Croc Experience. Awesome! I opened my mouth to ask more questions when the most horrible din burst through the windows that lined the end of the tropical house where we were standing.

Fingers started in shock. 'What the—'

Tori and I'd heard that noise before, but there was a more dangerous flavour to it today. It wasn't just anger we were hearing; it was pain and misery as well.

'The koalas!' Tori and I both cried at the same time.

We hurtled out of the tropical house, skidding back into the bitterness of the early morning. The growling had changed to a kind of spitting, but the awful sounds of despair seemed to be getting louder.

In the centre of the enclosure, the male koalas were heading back to the trees to lick their wounds. The bigger one had clearly won what had been a nasty battle full of claws and teeth. Arana was sitting stock-still in her tree, like she couldn't have cared less that blood had just been spilled on her behalf.

And Koko was lying on the ground, bloody and motionless, with Caramel the kangaroo squealing in distress beside her matted, pale-grey little body.

11

Judging Stuff on Appearances

Sasha and Paul both bolted out of the marsupial house. From their overalls it looked like they'd been preparing breakfast for the animals.

'Call Dr Nikolaides, the vet!' Sasha ordered Paul at once. She unbolted the gate with sure fingers and ran in to kneel beside Koko. The other animals in the enclosure were making nervous noises, the kangaroos hopping a safe distance away, the quokkas chattering a bit, and the wombats growling quietly. Caramel was still squealing. It was the most horrible sound. Up in her tree, Arana munched on.

'Is Koko dead?' Tori gulped.

'No. But she's badly injured.' Sasha was grim-faced. 'It looks like she got caught up in the koala fight.'

Caramel was rocking from side to side beside Koko, loudly and visibly upset. Sasha made soothing noises. 'Shh now, your little friend is going to be fine . . .'

We didn't know that, though. No one knew that.

Paul came running out of the office. 'Dr Nikolaides will be here in about ten minutes. He said to keep her as comfortable as possible until then.'

Tori started forward. 'Can we help?'

'I could fetch Mum,' I hiccuped, wiping my eyes. 'She'll know what to do.'

Sasha pushed her hands through her green-dyed hair. 'Thanks, girls, but we'd better not move her without Dr Nik. Oh, Koko!' she said, looking at the sad little bundle on the ground. 'Why weren't you safely up the tree with your mother?'

Paul got down to the business of netting Caramel so he could give her a mild sedative to calm her. He then went after the two male koalas, who had a few cuts and scratches but nothing that wouldn't heal by itself.

The same couldn't be said of Koko. Even from where we were standing, we could see a cut in the baby koala's side that was spilling blood on the ground. Sasha tenderly draped a blanket over the koala's little body to protect her from the bone-busting cold. She would need an operation, stitches – if she survived at all.

Arana had barely glanced at the madness surrounding her injured baby and was still sitting in her tree with her mouth full of eucalyptus leaves. I slid to the ground in a shocked and trembly heap.

'Why doesn't Arana care?' I howled into my fingers.

Tori sank down beside me and patted my shoulder. 'She's just not a natural mother, I suppose.'

'But Koko's her *baby*!'

And then Fingers was standing there and helping me back on to my feet, and Dr Nik appeared and Koko was swiftly examined, put into a little cage, and tucked securely into the vet's car.

'I'll take you back home,' said Fingers as we watched Dr Nik's car rushing towards the Wild World medical unit. 'There's nothing more we can do now except wait.'

Back at home, not even the sight of Toothy squeaking and clattering his teeth in welcome distracted me from the horribleness of what had just happened. As Fingers explained, Dad went green and disappeared off to his study at the back of the house, muttering about paperwork for a film about weasels that he'd been working on. He's rubbish with blood, which is a bit useless as he has to check his own umpteen times a day with this special pricker thing because of his diabetes. Wordlessly, Mum put the kettle on and made tea for everyone, giving me and Tori some extra spoons of sugar for the shock.

The sugar whizzed right to the tips of my fingers and made me tingle all over. I'm naturally a very positive person, so by about halfway through my tea I had convinced myself that Koko wasn't nearly as badly injured as she had looked. I'd once knocked my eyebrow against the bathroom cabinet; the cut had been teensy but the amount of blood made it look like someone had just given me a brain transplant. That's what had happened with Koko for sure.

'Koko will be fine,' I said. 'We'll get a phone call any minute telling us she's scampering around the unit and using Dr Nik's jacket pocket as a pouch.'

'It looked really bad,' Tori said in despair.

You know that glass-half-full, glass-half-empty thing that divides the optimists from the pessimists of this world? Tori's glass never even gets to the kitchen tap to begin with.

'We can't go round judging stuff on appearances,' I

said firmly. I put down my empty mug. 'I think we should all get busy and time will fly and the phone will ring and ta-da! We can all get on with our day, including Koko and Caramel and Arana.'

'Sitting and thinking about all the bad things won't help anyone – least of all Koko,' Fingers agreed. 'Taya, why don't you give Toothy some more food, help take your minds off all this for a while? He's been chirping like a little green bird ever since you came through the door.'

I smiled at Toothy, who smiled back with all two hundred of his little white teeth. He shuffled his splayed toes on his rock like he was doing some kind of scaly tap-dance routine.

'You had better do the same for Sarah-Jane,' Mum reminded Fingers.

Fingers got up. 'Thanks for the tea, Anita. Let me know when you hear any news about the young koala. Stay positive now! I'll come back later, see how Toothy's getting on.'

'Pinkies are in the animal fridge outside in the garage, Taya,' Mum said when Fingers had gone.

I don't want to creep you out, but pinkies are a special type of food that you can get for reptiles. They're basically hairless baby mice. Sorry, but they are. I fetched a few and brought them back inside. Toothy chomped them up with delight.

I was sliding the lid back over the top of his tank when the phone rang. Tori and I both rushed to pick up but Mum got there first.

'Jonas! How is little Koko? We have been so worried . . . Ah! Good! Yes, we must hope so . . . Yes . . . Yes, I will tell them. Goodbye.'

Replacing the receiver, Mum turned to us as we stood there, frozen with hope. 'The operation went well and Koko is all stitched up,' she said. 'She's still asleep from the anaesthetic, but she will hopefully wake up soon.'

'Yay!' I shouted. Punching the air, I swung round to Tori. 'I *told* you it would be OK, didn't I?'

'What did you mean when you said that bit about "We must hope so" to Dr Nik, Mum?' Tori asked.

'Koko is very young to undergo an operation like this,' Mum explained. 'Her body may still go into shock, or she may not come round from the anaesthetic. There will be several more days of recovery before anyone can be sure she will survive.'

All I was hearing were Doom and his best mate Gloom. Didn't anyone in this house know how to enjoy good news?

'Come *on*, guys!' I waved my hands in the air like an excited Italian lady. 'Stay positive, remember? Can we go and visit Koko, Mum?'

'Dr Nik won't want visitors just yet,' Mum warned.

'We'll go up there anyway,' Tori suggested, looking at me. 'Rabbit needs a walk.'

The morning had brightened quite a lot by the time we'd put on coats and scarves and hats, and clipped on Rabbit's lead, and stepped out of the front door for the second time that day. It still wasn't exactly warm, but my nose took at least ten minutes of walking to turn into an ice pop. The Wild World doors had opened, so a number of brave members of the public with red noses and large hats were milling about, peering at the animals and stamping their feet on the chilly ground. The café and its fantastic hot chocolate would do a roaring trade today.

'Caramel will be *so* relieved,' I said happily as we turned the corner and headed up one last bit of hill to the medical unit. 'I wish I could speak kangaroo, then I could tell her the good news myself. Dr Nik's a brilliant vet, isn't he?'

Tori just stuck her hands a bit deeper into her pockets and didn't reply.

'Oh, don't tell me,' I said. 'You're picturing how Koko will maybe stop breathing in between the phone call and us getting to the unit. I'm right, aren't I?'

'I just like to be *sure* before I get happy, OK?' Tori said, all defensive. 'There's nothing wrong with that.'

We both stopped and waited for Rabbit, who'd stuck her whole head inside a bush and was wagging her rear end so hard she was practically knocking herself off her own four feet. That was when I heard it.

'Tor,' I said slowly, 'did you—'

'—hear that special squeak that Toothy makes?' Tori finished my question for me with round eyes. 'Yes, I did.'

We were nowhere near Sarah-Jane and the tropical house. And even if we'd been standing right outside the tropical-house doors, the chances of hearing a baby crocodile squeaking all the way from the back of the building were slim to none.

I heard it again. This time I looked down.

With one foot raised in the air, his head tilted to one side, his little jaws open and his tail twitching on the frosty grass verge, Toothy was looking right at me as if to say, 'It's about time you noticed.'

12

Perfectly Simple Explanation

'*Toothy!*' I was practically fossilized with the shock of seeing the little crocodile. 'What are you *doing*?'

Down on the verge, Toothy swapped feet and lifted his other one up for a bit, probably to warm it up. His big green eyes didn't waver for a second.

'How did he get here?' I stuttered in bewilderment. 'I put the lid on his ta . . .'

A faint memory of dashing for the phone in the middle of replacing the tank-lid floated into my brain. Clearly, I hadn't finished the job.

'Tank,' I finished in a small voice.

'Taya, you total idiot!' Tori breathed. 'Mum'll be *furious*!'

Crocodiles are unbelievably amazing creatures.

Toothy had hatched only hours ago, and yet here he was, miles away from where he was supposed to be, having escaped from his tank, made it through the front door without Mum seeing, and followed us all the way through the park. If these guys evolved any further, the human race would be in serious trouble.

Toothy made a sudden dash towards us. Before I could react he had hopped on to the toe of my boot, where it was a bit warmer than the icy ground.

Oh my wombats, there was a crocodile on my boot. Now the shock was fading a bit, the next stage was a terrible flood of giggles.

'Oh, oh,' I gasped, trying to laugh as quietly as I possibly could at this insane situation. 'Oh, Toothy . . .'

Toothy gazed up at me, unmoved by the tears of laughter that were squeezing out of my eyes. Which of course made the whole thing even funnier.

'Pick him up!' Tori ordered, glancing around. 'Quickly, before he runs off and freaks out half the park!'

I could hardly bend down, I was laughing so much. 'Pick him . . . up for me, Tor . . . I . . . I can't . . .'

'He'll bite me, so it has to be you!' Tori hissed. 'Snap out of it, Taya!'

Well, of all the things to say.

'*Snap*,' I moaned. 'And he's a . . . a . . . crocodile . . .'

A voice floated towards us, thick with curiosity.

'Does that girl have a *crocodile* on her boot, Stuart?'

Two park visitors started coming closer in that nosy-human sort of way. Tori pinched me hard in a desperate attempt to bring me to my senses. I took several deep gasping breaths, practically burning my lungs out in the freezing air. Then I bent down and grabbed the little croc behind his neat green front legs. He squeaked in my arms with his jaws open in his usual crocodile smile.

'We'll have to take him home,' said Tori urgently. 'It's too cold for him outside. *And don't let anyone see!*'

I quickly opened my coat and tucked Toothy inside. It wasn't a minute too soon.

'Ask her, Stuart. Ask her! I swear I saw a crocodile!'

'Excuse me . . .' The man visitor looked hesitant. 'Was there – I mean, my wife wondered – was there a crocodile on your boot just now?'

'A crocodile?' Tori turned to me. 'Did you just have a crocodile on your boot, Taya?'

'No crocodiles here,' I lied. Toothy was moving around under my coat so I folded my arms to cover up the wriggling.

The nosy lady's eyes narrowed. 'I saw it on your boot.'

Tori looked at my boot. So did I. So did the nosy lady's husband and the nosy lady herself. We all gazed at my boot like it was going to break into some sort of explanation all by itself; like the sole was going to peel away from the leather bit on the top and start saying: 'Right, well, the thing is, there *was* a crocodile sitting on me just now, but there's a perfectly simple explanation . . .'

'Maybe it was a leaf,' said Tori, looking up again.

'Oh yes, I *did* just have a leaf on my boot!' I amaze myself with the lies I come up with sometimes. 'A sort of long green crinkly leaf. It came from, um . . .' My frantic eyes lit on the bush Rabbit was still trying to wreck. 'That bush.'

The park visitors' eyes swivelled to the bush in question. Miraculously, it *did* have long crinkly greenish leaves. One or two were even lying helpfully on the ground near Rabbit's waggling back end.

A leaf on a boot is a lot more likely than a crocodile, on the whole.

'A leaf. Of course. Our mistake,' the man said hurriedly. 'It was a ridiculous question and I rather wish I hadn't asked it now. You must think we're mad!

Come on, Lesley. Sorry to have bothered you, girls.'

We waited as they walked off. We could still hear the wife hissing at her embarrassed husband about knowing crocodiles when she saw them, however unlikely.

When they were out of sight, Tori and I breathed out and stared at each other. I could feel a fresh round of hysterics building in my gut that I knew would be *way* worse than the first lot. Then Toothy's icy little body found a warm, bare bit of skin between the bottom of my jumper and the top of my jeans and stopped my giggles in their tracks.

'AIEEEEEEEEE!'

Tori leaped out of her skin. Rabbit leaped further into the bush. Thank wombats the nosy couple were out of hearing because there was absolutely no way I would have survived another round of questions.

'Sorry,' I said helplessly. 'He's cold!'

Tori shook her head to show how juvenile she thought I was as my giggles returned in a seriously major way. My sister's such a blinking *grown-up*.

'You know something?' she said after a while, as I gasped and howled and wiped my eyes with the hand which wasn't clutching Toothy inside my coat. 'I think Rabbit's stuck in that bush.'

When I'd caught my breath, I helped my twin to haul our grateful, wheezing, twig-covered dog out of the Wild World shrubbery. We took the shortest route home that we could think of, postponing our visit to Koko, who was probably still zonked with the anaesthetic anyway and not up to visitors just yet. Toothy snuggled a bit closer to my warm tummy, but I didn't yell out a second time. Frankly I was too knackered.

Who says there's no such thing as too much laughter?

13

Making WHAAT? Faces

Mum met us at the front door with a wild look in her eyes. Behind her, we could see that the house had been turned upside down. Cushions were strewn around the sitting room; cupboards had been emptied. Dad was pacing around the kitchen, nervously checking underneath the fridge and the kitchen table. He'd put his outdoor shoes on, probably in case Toothy fancied a bit of human toe for lunch. Toothy's tank sat looking at us on its airing-cupboard shelf, empty and accusing.

'*Queridas!*' Mum gasped. 'We have bad news. Toothy—'

'—is just fine, Mum,' I said awkwardly. I produced the little crocodile from inside my coat. 'He's right here.'

'He followed us through the park,' Taya added.

Mum made a deflating noise and sank down on one of the kitchen chairs with her hand pressed over her heart. Dad took his shoes off again and wiggled his socky feet with relief.

There was no way out of this, so I jumped right in.

'It was my fault,' I confessed. 'I didn't put the lid of his tank on properly.'

Mum was about to give me a rocket; I could tell from the way her chocolate eyes had started to smoulder. But Dad – lovely, chilled Dad – jumped in and saved me.

'There's no point in yelling, Anita love. Toothy's back safely, no one saw, no harm done.'

Tori grimaced. 'Someone did see, actually.'

'But we persuaded them that they were imagining things,' I put in, sliding Toothy back into his tank and pushing the lid on as tightly as I could. 'So you don't have to worry about that.'

The phone rang out in the hall and Tori went to pick up. She handed the receiver to Mum. 'It's Fingers,' she said solemnly. 'He knows.'

Oh wombats.

Mum fixed me with a flaming gaze. 'I think perhaps you had better explain all this to him, Taya, hmm?'

I took the phone nervously. 'Um – hi, Fingers . . .'

Fingers sounded very worried. 'A reporter from *The Fernleigh Post* rang Matt about ten minutes ago to say that a lady had contacted him with news of a dangerous reptile on the loose in the park in the company of two young girls. Please don't tell me you took Toothy for a walk, Taya!'

Dangerous reptile? Toothy was barely the same length as my school ruler!

'He escaped and followed us!' I wailed. The giggles of half an hour ago were a long-distant memory. 'But he's safely back in his tank again now. I'm really, *really* sorry, Fingers.'

'And he's OK?' Fingers checked.

'He got a bit cold, but he's perked up now,' I said, glancing at where Toothy was paddling up and down in his tank like he didn't have a care in the world.

There was a pause. I could practically hear Fingers's brain whirring on the other end of the phone. 'Right, let's turn this into something useful,' he said at last. 'Taya, how would you like to do a newspaper interview?'

I almost dropped the phone. Mum, Dad and Tori, who were trying to follow the conversation without giving away the fact that they were trying to follow the conversation, all looked startled.

'A newspaper interview?' I repeated in dismay, making WHAAT? faces at my family. 'You want me to apologize in the local paper for letting Toothy escape?'

Fingers sounded amused. 'Why not? Everyone loves a good apology. We could drum up a great bit of publicity. I'll double-check with Matt and then we'll ask the reporter over for a chat tomorrow, shall we?'

Silently I passed the phone to Mum, who got into an enthusiastic conversation with Fingers at once about launching some new reptile awareness programme for Wild World on the back of my public humiliation.

'They say there's no such thing as bad publicity,' Dad offered sympathetically.

I pictured my classmates reading all about my mistake in the paper. They'd laugh for *weeks*. Tori was already smirking and the thing hadn't even been written yet.

'Guess what?' I muttered through my fingers. 'They're wrong.'

And here's another guessing game for you. Who had to tidy up the whole house after Mum and Dad's crazed attempt at finding Toothy? Yup. Got it in one. Naturally Tori didn't offer to help. She just disappeared upstairs to do her maths homework. *Quel* swot.

Matt approved the idea of the interview and on Sunday morning I was put through the hideous experience of telling a complete stranger what a doughnut I was. I flew at it the way they always say you should deal with a plaster on a cut – rip it off in one go. The reporter only interrupted a couple of times, checking one or two crocodile facts and making sure he'd spelled the word 'imprinting' right, before taking some close-up photos of me with Fingers and Toothy sitting on my shoulder. (Only Toothy was sitting on my shoulder, obviously.) We even managed to get a bit of a mention for Dad's film business, Wild About Animals. But it was still quite possibly the most embarrassing experience of my entire life. The article was going to be published in *The Fernleigh Post* on Tuesday and the whole thing had got everyone in a frenzy of excitement.

I didn't mention Toothy to a single soul on Monday, not even Joe or Biro, even when Joe asked if the eggs had hatched yet. Luckily the whole class's attention was focused on Cazza's surprisingly quiet and harmonious return. She had sat silently beside Tori all afternoon and hadn't even spat on the floor once.

Back at home, I put up with an evening of Mum,

Fingers and Matt all banging on over Mum's best shepherd's pie about Wild World's plans for major reptile research and conservation and how the article might even be taken up by the national press. Toothy had chattered loudly from his tank at that bit, like he'd understood what they were talking about. Terrific. As if local humiliation wasn't enough, we were now talking *nationwide* levels of embarrassment. Dad spent his time bustling around in the kitchen and throwing in helpful remarks along the lines of, 'Have you shut the fridge, Taya? Can you check the front door is properly closed?' The only good bit of the evening was a call from Dr Nik to say that Koko was showing signs of recovering from her fight ordeal and operation, and that we could come for a visit in the next couple of days if we wanted to.

'I'm so pleased that everyone's happy,' I said bitterly as Tori and I settled down to sleep to the sounds of grown-up laughter still ringing around downstairs. 'They're not the ones who'll get all the crocodile jokes in the morning.'

'What's a crocodile's favourite game?' teased Tori.

'Happy Families,' I snarled.

14

Did You Leave the Fridge Door Open Again?

I awoke to a sparkly new world of fame.

Dad got the local paper delivered on a Tuesday morning. The moment my eyes snapped open, I hurtled down the stairs and grabbed the rolled-up paper from the letterbox. Toothy and I were front-page news.

At first this seemed like the worst possible result. Now there was no *way* half the class might miss the fact that I was in the paper! Groaning and trying to formulate a reason for not going to school today – pneumonia? broken nose? dead? – I took a handful of biscuits from the cupboard to fortify myself before reading. Rabbit climbed out of her basket and sat beside me, panting heavily. Early visitors to the kitchen usually meant early breakfast for the dog.

It was quite a good picture of me. My hair, which is long and brown and quite boring, actually looked shiny and with a bit of a curl on the ends. Toothy looked extremely cute, sitting on my shoulder and peering at the camera with his jaws open like he was about to nosh on my earlobe.

I scanned the words. *Wild World wildlife park . . . Nile crocodile eggs . . . all-night vigil for the eggs to hatch . . . accidental imprinting . . . pushed the lid off his tank and followed her into the park . . .*

Hang on. *Pushed* his lid off? But hadn't . . . Didn't . . . ?

I read the rest of the article with growing amazement. This wasn't an apology. It was practically a love letter!

Taya Wild is a bright, bubbly girl . . .

Taya is very knowledgeable about reptiles for her age . . .

Taya Wild shows remarkable maturity . . .

There was other stuff about Toothy and Wild World too, obviously, but those bits didn't matter. What mattered was that, instead of embarrassing me, the article had made me sound unbelievably cool!

Toothy called me from his tank.

'I'm famous, Toothy!' I told him with delight. 'Wahoo!'

I dashed up the stairs, waving the article in the air like a victory flag.

'MUM! DAD! TORIIIIII! You have to read this!'

Mum came out of the bathroom. 'Do they give a lot of attention to our new reptile programme?' she asked eagerly. 'We asked the reporter specially . . .'

I pressed the paper into Mum's hands. 'See what it says about me being all knowledgeable? And it said I was bubbly. And see how nice my hair looks!'

'There is not as much information about our conservation work as I was hoping,' Mum said, reading the paper with a frown. 'But it is a start, I suppose.'

Still wearing his pyjamas, Dad peered at the article over Mum's shoulder. 'Ooh, good – Wild About Animals gets a whole paragraph!' he said. 'The weasel film project is winding up now and we could do with more work. Maybe this will drum up some fresh business.'

'Read what it says about *me*!' I insisted. 'Look! I bet you never knew you had such a cool daughter.'

'Very cool,' said Dad, ruffling my head. 'Did you leave the fridge door open again?'

Well, my parents were a *right* pair of useless twits. I

snatched the paper from Mum's hands and charged on up the stairs to our room to show Tori.

I should have known better than to expect any praise from my twin, of course. Tori read the article slowly and carefully, giving my photo one swift glance. Then she laid it down on the bed and went back to brushing her hair without saying a single word.

'How brilliant is that?' I prompted.

'I thought it would say more about Fingers's work with reptile conservation,' Tori answered.

'I'm going to take it to school and show everyone,' I said, undeterred by my sister's determination to give me zero credit. 'Hey, maybe I should carry it on the bus face-out and see how many people recognize me without me saying anything!' I shot a glance at the mirror and tilted my head a little, trying to conjure up the same smile I'd done for the article.

'Maybe you should take Toothy to school as well,' said Tori. 'Have him on your shoulder all day long. Then everyone will know it's you for sure.'

'That would be pretty awesome,' I said dreamily. 'Only Mum wouldn't let me in a million years.'

Tori made a spluttering noise. 'I'm *joking*, Taya! Did you seriously think I meant it?'

'There's no need to be all sarky just because it's me

in the paper and not you,' I snapped, flushing.

Tori did up her tie and straightened her skirt. 'We're identical twins, you doofus,' she pointed out. 'I'll probably get noticed just the same as you. *If* I cared, which I completely don't.'

I hate my sister sometimes. She knows exactly how to rain on my parade.

'Taya! Did you feed Rabbit?' Mum called from downstairs.

'No!' I called back, taking off my PJs and wriggling sulkily into my pants.

'What about Toothy?'

'Nope! I was reading my article, remember?'

'Some mother you are,' said Tori, walking out of the bedroom and heading down for breakfast.

I got my revenge on my sister at school that morning.

'Have you read the end bit yet, Cazza? About how if you want to see the baby crocs before they get much bigger, you'd better make it snappy?' I gave a tinkling laugh. 'Well hilarious, that bit. He's a brilliant reporter, isn't he?'

Cazza's eyes were wide and impressed as she read my article. A cluster of other kids gathered around behind us: Cash 'n' Carrie, Tosh and Jonno, Biro, Joe, and pretty much the entire class. Tori sat stiffly beside me, trying to write something on the worksheet Ms Hutson had handed out.

'That's wicked, Taz babe,' Cazza said, whistling through her teeth. 'A pet crocodile! How hard are you?' She punched me in admiration, giving me a dead arm by mistake.

'He's not a pet,' said Tori sharply.

Cazza flapped a hand in my twin's direction. 'Chill, Tor. Your sister's, like, a celebrity! With a crocodile!'

Tori's eyes narrowed. She doesn't like being flapped at.

'I expect the national papers will take the story too,' I said carelessly. 'It's not every day you see a kid with a crocodile, is it?'

'So is this crocodile still living in your house, Taya?' asked Heather Cashman.

Carrie gave a squeal, part disgust and part envy.

'Can we come and see it?' Jonno Nkobe put in. 'Can we stroke it?'

'Toothy would bite you,' I explained. 'Sorry, Jonno. But you can come to Wild World any time you like. I could talk to my mum about getting you on some kind of VIP list, maybe.'

Beside me, Tori snorted.

'7H!' Ms Hutson said from the front of the class. She sounded exasperated. 'This is all very interesting, but we have work to do. Back to your seats, please!'

Everyone shuffled reluctantly back to their desks. Cazza stayed where she was, still staring at the newspaper.

'Toothy,' she said, and laughed. 'You named him after 2thi, then?'

I nodded proudly.

Cazza leaned a bit closer to me. 'Can I tell you a secret about 2thi?'

I felt flattered and a bit scared at the same time. Cazza close up was more alarming than Cazza at a normal distance. I could still see the little hole in her nose where her parents had made her take out her zigzag stud.

'We're related,' said Cazza, watching me carefully for my reaction.

My jaw flopped open. 'What? You and the rapper?'

'It's not like official or anything,' Cazza added, glancing over her shoulder like the relation police were about to bust her. 'But I swear, he's my cousin maybe. Dunno for sure because it's all, like, totally top secret and that. But – well, you gotta see the resemblance.'

I thought very hard about the way 2thi looked. Then

I thought about Cazza. Maybe their chins matched? I didn't know about eyes because 2thi always wore sunglasses. And I didn't know about hair either because Caz dyed hers and 2thi shaved his off in all these zigzag patterns so the real colour was hard to see. Cazza had tried to get a nose stud like the rapper's and talked a bit like he did. She liked 2thi's music and I figured 2thi probably liked 2thi's music too, seeing how he wrote and performed it. Apart from that, I couldn't see any resemblance at all. But I nodded obediently because Cazza had told me a secret and it was important to respect this if I didn't want my face torn off.

Cazza sat back, looking pleased. 'We're dead ringers,' she said in satisfaction. 'And there's no *way* that's coincidence. I'll find out the truth for myself one day, you'll see. No one can keep stuff like that a secret for ever, right?'

15

Indigestion City

'I'm going to visit Koko after school today,' Tori told me at lunch. 'You coming?'

My head was so full of fortune and fame and Cazza's little revelation that it took me a couple of seconds to work out who Koko was.

'What? Oh, the koala!'

Tori looked at me. 'No, the elephant that Dr Nik has got recuperating in the medical unit.'

I stared at my sister in some astonishment. 'Wild World has a sick *elephant*?'

Tori made a tsking noise, picked up her tray and took it over to the dirty trays bit. I still had a bit of my jacket potato to go, but I tried to wolf it down quickly so I could follow. Oh boy – indigestion city.

Cazza tweaked my sleeve from the other side of the table just as I'd stuffed the last bit of spud in my mouth.

'You didn't tell about me and 2thi, did you?' she asked in a low voice.

'Fufufuf,' I promised through my mouthful of potato, equally low.

'Right,' she said with a nod. 'Cool. 'Cause you know something? I haven't even told Tori and she's, like, my best mate.'

I swallowed, my eyes burning a bit. Tori was already halfway to the canteen door and I really wanted to talk to her about that weird stuff she'd just said about an elephant. Cazza was still looking at me. If she hadn't been Cazza, I'd have said she seemed nervous.

'Why haven't you told Tori then?' I asked.

Cazza looked gloomy. 'She'd say I'm nuts. Not like you.'

I felt pleased. 'Yeah, I believe most things until someone proves different,' I assured her.

'Sick,' said Cazza, though I wasn't sure if this was a good thing or not.

'Are you finished?' I asked. 'Wanna go and find Tori?'

Cazza grabbed her tray. 'You're sworn to, like, silence, Taz,' she warned.

Like silence? I *hate* silence.

'I won't tell *anyone*,' I promised with all my heart.

Well. As if life wasn't already pretty good, things got *really* exciting the moment Tori and I turned in through our garden gate after school.

Mum flung open the front door.

'We are going to the whole country, *queridas*! Matt's phone had been ringing off the hoop all day and our story will be in the national newspapers tomorrow morning!'

I squealed. I actually squealed, like a mouse or a bat or just a really, really excited person.

'Off the *hook*, Mum,' Tori said, dumping her school bag in the porch. She aimed for the fridge and a large glass of milk before disappearing up the stairs.

I was still squealing, with Mum squealing right alongside me. She grabbed me and waltzed the two of us around the kitchen, our hair spinning out behind us. Rabbit retreated behind the sofa while Toothy watched us with his ancient, unblinking eyes from behind the glassy walls of his tank.

'This is a personal dwelling not a Justin Bieber concert,' Dad bellowed through the wall of the room he was using as a study. 'I can't hear myself *think*!'

'OK,' I gulped, still fizzing like an enthusiastic can of Fanta as Mum and I stopped spinning and collapsed on to a pair of kitchen chairs. 'OK, OK, I'm calm. I'm calm. Mum, calm down . . .' *I was going national!*

'Wild World is going national!' Mum cried. 'We must put systems in place for fundraising – perhaps we can do a special hotwire phone for donations . . . Fingers! I must tell him right away!'

Mum sprang up from her chair and raced for the phone. I closed my eyes and imagined my huge and glorious future. Newspapers. TV, even. Oh boy oh boy oh boy.

Toothy scraped on his tank with a claw to get some attention.

'I'll feed you in a minute, babes,' I said, my head in an extremely happy place.

Tori came back downstairs in jeans and a sweatshirt. 'You coming?' she asked me, reaching for her coat.

I still had my eyes closed. 'Where?'

The next thing I knew, the front door had closed and Tori hadn't answered my question. I had no idea what my sister was up to. Being a geek as usual, probably.

I fetched Toothy some of his pinkies and watched him dreamily as he tore each one to shreds. 'I'm loving every moment of this as much as you're loving your pinkies,' I told him.

Then I dashed upstairs. I had a wardrobe to plan.

'La la la,' I sang, waltzing down the garden path on Wednesday afternoon with my hands over my ears.

Mr Collyer had read out my article from a national newspaper in assembly today and the whole school had said nice things to me all day long apart from a couple of jokers in Year Ten who'd jumped at me in the corridor right at the end of the day with their arms clapping shut, yelling 'SNAP!' at the tops of their voices and practically sending Joe through the ceiling with fright.

'They're just, like, jealous,' said Cazza when we'd scraped Joe back together.

'Best joke ever,' Tori'd gasped, holding her sides.

So I wasn't really talking to her just then, hence the singing thing.

'Fine,' she now said angrily, a few paces behind me on the path. She'd been waffling on about something that I'd refused to listen to ever since we'd got off our bus. 'I'm getting changed and going up to the medical unit and you and your mad fame obsession can get stuffed.'

I made a W sign with my fingers which I'd seen on a movie once. It means 'Whatever!' and is perhaps the most annoying thing anyone can do to you, which was why I enjoyed doing it to my sister so much.

'Hi, Dad!' I sang, pirouetting through the kitchen as Tori stormed upstairs. 'Have there been any calls for me?'

Dad was holding the phone and scratching his beard with his free hand. 'Not for you, Taya – no. But I've had an interesting one for Wild About Animals.'

I selected a biscuit from the tin and went over to scratch Toothy on the head. 'Did they read about you in my article?'

Dad raised his eyebrows. 'They said they had seen *the* article, yes,' he said. 'It's for a music video.'

'Awesome!' I gasped. 'Who? Someone famous?'

'I can't say I've heard of him,' Dad confessed. 'But you might have. Some bloke called Toothy?'

16

Assistant's Assistant's Assistant

'OMG! OMG!' Cazza clutched my forearm so hard I had visions of it dropping off my elbow joint like a withered rose that's just been dead-headed. 'O. M. G!!!'

'Don't encourage her, Caz,' advised Tori from somewhere under the table, where she was rummaging in her bag for something nerdish like a pencil or a protractor. 'She's turning into a nightmare. Believe me, I've had it up to here—' her arm came up above the table top and stretched for the ceiling '—with this whole ego trip.'

'Just because you're jealous,' I said at once. Not *one* person had asked Tori about Toothy; so much for her theory about her getting half the fame because we look alike.

Tori gave a trumpety snort of disgust and, to my extreme delight, banged her head on the underside of the table.

Cash 'n' Carrie were standing beside me like a pair of hypnotized meerkats.

'Seriously?' breathed Heather Cashman, twisting her black curly hair extremely fast round her finger.

'Like, *see*riously?' Carrie echoed, reliable as very reliable clockwork. '2thi wants you in his video?'

'OMG,' repeated Cazza.

'Strictly speaking, 2thi wants *Toothy* in his video,' I corrected. 'But as I'm Toothy's surrogate mum, I've got to go to the filming because my little croc won't like it unless I'm there too.'

'But *why*?' Heather's hushed voice suggested aliens had beamed into Fernleigh and had decided to crown me their Earthly Queen for crazy alien reasons that were beyond explanation.

'2thi thought it was cute that I'd named Toothy after him.' It really is a cute name for a crocodile, don't you think? Better than Sarah-Jane any day. 'And it gave him an idea for his new music video. Simple really.'

'So are you going to meet him first?' Joe asked.

'He's coming to meet me, Toothy, my mum, my dad and Fingers, the keeper, this weekend,' I said, savouring the way everyone's impossibly wide eyes had somehow got even wider. 'At Wild World. I think he wants to do the filming ASAP.'

'Can we—' began Heather, but I lifted an arm to stop her.

'Sorry, Heather. He's dead funny about privacy. It's just going to be him, his manager, his assistant, his assistant's assistant, his assistant's assistant's assistant and a couple of other assistants. Really low key and anonymous. He won't want a bunch of little kids coming round to gawk at him.'

Heather twitched satisfyingly.

The bell went. Tori was already on her feet.

'Science now,' she announced. 'Anyone coming, or is Taya going to sign a few autographs first?'

Everyone grabbed their stuff.

'What are we doing today, anyway?' I asked, wondering if I could get away with not handing in my really bad Science homework because of my motherly duties with Toothy.

'I think it's a brain experiment,' Tori said as we all headed out of the room to join the tidal wave of bodies destined for their next bit of educational stuffing. 'We pick the biggest head in the class and dissect it.'

I was loading up my sarcasm catapult for the

perfect return shot when Cazza grabbed hold of my arm again and pulled me close. Her grip was even tighter than before.

'Taz!' Her eyes looked demented. More demented than normal I mean. 'Taz, man! Find out about his family! I gotta prove our connection and I don't have nothing to go on except our, like, total physical resemblance. Do it for me? Say you will?'

Dad fixed the meeting with 2thi for the weekend, so that I could be there and not miss any school. By all accounts, it hadn't been easy.

'You wouldn't believe the run-around these people have given me, and we haven't even met the man yet,' he moaned on Friday night. Mum dished up sympathetic ladles of soup and prodded me to fetch Dad another beer from the fridge. 'I've spoken to so many people claiming to represent Nigel Tinsel that for all I know I've just set up an entire conference.'

'Nigel Tinsel?' said Tori.

I felt panicky. 'Dad, we're supposed to be meeting a world-famous rapper, not the manager of the local Christmas Club!'

'Your 2thi fellow's real name is Nigel Tinsel,' Dad explained.

'Aiee,' said Mum. She's become English enough to know an uncool name when she hears one.

Tori burst into such wild laughter that Rabbit started barking at the back door. Rabbit's hearing is well up the spout, along with most of her limbs. My baby crocodile froze to his rock with one foot in the air like a tiny dragon statue doing the jive. 2thi's real name was Nigel Tinsel? I mean, *Tinsel*? Was that even a real name?

'Nigel Tinsel!' Tori hooted, clutching her stomach. 'Ti . . . Ti . . . nsel!'

'So anyway,' Dad went on, 'it's all fixed for tomorrow at ten. We've agreed to do it here, so that Toothy isn't overly disturbed. I don't suppose it'll last long.'

Tears of laughter were pouring down Tori's cheeks. 'Please . . . please may I be excused?' she hiccuped.

'If you've wet yourself, the laundry basket's in the bathroom,' I said, sweet as a sugar-coated dagger.

In the morning, Tori had recovered. In fact, she was looking positively jaunty.

'Have fun with Tinselpants, Taya,' she said, grabbing her coat and hat out of the porch. It was raining out, so she selected our biggest umbrella as well. 'I'm sure you'll sparkle. Get it? I'm going to visit Koko.'

I was bolting my toast so as to give myself more time for some serious pre-2thi preening. It was already eight-thirty; he was coming in *an hour and a half*. Eeek! 'Give Koko a kiss from me!' I said generously, swallowing half a bit of toast in one go.

'Remembered who she is, have you?' Tori enquired. 'Yes, she's looked a little better both times that I've been to visit her, thanks for asking, but we're not out of the eucalyptus trees yet. What's that? How's Caramel coping? Well, she's been off her food all week and has lost three kilos, which is way too much. See you later.'

I brushed the crumbs rather slowly off the front of my dressing-gown when Tori'd gone. A picture of little bleeding Koko stuck itself on top of the spangly visions I'd been having about me and Nigel '2thi' Tinsel. And poor Caramel. I felt a side-swipe of guilt clonk me round the chops as I thought about the way she'd rocked from side to side when Koko was hurt. I'd barely given her or Koko a second thought since the newspaper article.

The phone rang. Dad grabbed it.

'What? Yes? Mr . . . ? Have we spoken before? No, no, I didn't think we had . . . Noon, you say?' Dad rolled his eyes at me. 'Yes, twelve noon will be fine.

Yes. Thanks. See you then.' He put the receiver back on the cradle. 'Good news, Taya,' he informed me. 'You now have three and a half hours to get ready before our visitation. I'd better let Fingers know we've been delayed.'

'Cool,' I said, feeling relieved. There's only so much primping a girl can do in an hour and a half.

I wondered if I should maybe go after Tori and see how Koko was getting on. Then I thought about the frosty reception I would get from my twin and changed my mind. Koko would be fine, I reassured myself. Dr Nik was looking after her, wasn't he? How many visitors did one little koala need? Anyway, I needed a bit of serious thinking time, to dream up a way of asking 2thi what Cazza so desperately wanted me to ask. It was mental, this idea that Cazza and 2thi were related, but Cazza was so convinced that maybe – just maybe – there was something in it. She *was* adopted, after all.

'*Now we're done talking about crocodiles, let's talk about your family, Mr Tinsel . . .*'

I went upstairs to ponder this beneath a blasting-hot shower with my new bananas-and-cream shower gel. For some reason, I found it hard to concentrate.

17

Baldy Zigzags

Nigel '2thi' Tinsel turned up at half past four, along with what felt like about thirty-five other people, most of whom were wearing sunglasses even though it was already dark outside. It was a bit of a squeeze round the kitchen table. Rabbit took one look, weighed up the chances of getting her tail trodden on, and headed for the sitting-room sofa.

After ignoring my tentative questions about how Koko was doing, Tori'd gone out to meet Cazza in town soon after she got back from the medical unit. She still wasn't back. Now I stared at my lap and smoothed my best purple skirt down for the millionth time since I'd put it on that morning. I was getting seriously bored of looking at it. Toothy was snoozing on his rock in the cupboard with the door open, Mum standing guard beside him.

'So, Mr Tinsel—' Dad began.

'My client prefers his stage name, Mr Wild,' interrupted a tall, tanned guy with slicked blond hair – 2thi's manager, I guessed.

Once I'd got over the shock of 2thi actually being in my kitchen, I had started searching his face – at least, those bits of his face that I could see round the edges of his massive sunglasses – for some kind of Cazza likeness. The rapper was pale and a bit pock-marked, and the hair that I could see around the baldy zigzags carved on his skull was a sort of mousy-brown colour. His famous zigzag nose stud glinted in the kitchen lights and his whole body shimmered in the glittery tracksuit he was wearing. *Take off your sunnies*, I prayed.

'Mr 2thi, then,' said Dad politely. 'Tell us about your plans and how we can help you.'

2thi shifted on his chair and didn't say anything. He looked utterly bored.

'My client is having a jungle theme for the video of his new single, "Down Wiv U",' said the manager.

Dad was writing busily. 'Spelled . . . ?'

The manager spelled the song. I squirmed for Tori and her loathing of dumb spellings. *Tori*. What was I thinking about her for? 2thi was in my kitchen, drinking coffee out of one of Mum's best mugs, for wombat's sake!

As Dad, Fingers and 2thi's manager got into a conversation about the practicalities of taking Toothy up to London for the shoot, 2thi himself suddenly spoke.

'Let's see this croc with my name then,' he said. His voice was a bit squeaky.

Everyone stared at the open airing cupboard. Toothy stared back. Talk about unbothered. That crocodile had sussed everyone in the room already and decided they were deeply uninteresting. I had a strong urge to giggle.

Pulling himself out of his chair with a loud jangle of jewellery, 2thi went over to the airing cupboard for a close-up. Mum looked as if she was flexing her fingers, preparing to thwack him if he reached into the tank.

'You might see him better if you took off your sunglasses,' Fingers suggested.

There were a few intakes of breath around the room. Clearly, no one ever suggested stuff like that to their boss. But 2thi slid his sunnies on to the top of his head obediently and peered into the tank. Toothy did his hypnotic 'I may be only thirty centimetres long but inside I'm a T-Rex' look. The rapper turned back to his posse and grinned, flashing the two pointed gold incisors that gave him his stage name. His eyes disappeared from view as the sunglasses went back on and he came back to the table.

His eyes were a very pale blue. Nothing like Cazza's black ones at all.

Fingers launched into more specifics with Dad and 2thi's manager – how he would be coming along to the video shoot and how it was his duty to ensure Toothy wouldn't be put in any dangerous or uncomfortable situations in compliance with animal protection regulations . . . I tried to concentrate on the conversation but I kept coming back to Cazza and 2thi. How was I going to face her on Monday if I didn't somehow ask about the rapper's family? This was a major chance to talk to him and I was sitting here like a lemon!

'. . . and Taya here has agreed to come as well, to minimize the stress for the young crocodile.'

Everyone now stared at me, much in the same way they'd stared at the airing cupboard. I had no idea what they'd just said. So I responded with the question that just happened to be lolloping through my brain at that particular moment in time.

'Tinsel's an interesting name. Is it, er – Icelandish?'

There was a shocked pause.

Well, I'd started now. So I persevered. 'You see, we've been looking at unusual surnames and talking about families and *adoptions*' – I put extra-special stress on the word adoptions – 'and stuff at school lately so I thought I'd ask.'

I looked expectantly at 2thi. He seemed to be struggling with something.

'My dad's German,' he said at last, in a cautious sort of voice. 'And I ain't adopted, if that's what you're asking, kid.'

German. I filed this away, relieved that I had something to tell Cazza.

'What were you saying about me, anyway?' I asked brightly, gazing around at the rest of the table.

The conversation got back on track. Towards the end, 2thi suddenly became really animated. He thumped the table and dented the surface with one of his huge gold rings. 'I wanna go all out here. Proper jungle. It's gotta be dangerous. It's gotta be real. It's gotta have impact. We'll have a full-size croc in the shoot as well as this little guy. Yeah, a proper beast! The world's gonna go *mental* when they see it!'

2thi's posse started nodding and fist-bumping around the table.

'A full-grown crocodile on set?' Fingers shot an alarmed look at Mum and Dad. 'I wouldn't recommend it.'

2thi tapped his nose with a pointy gold grin. 'I hear you, no sweat. Just get this little guy where he's supposed to be. I'm bored with this now, bro,' he said, turning to his manager. 'I'm gonna shoot.'

The rapper got to his feet and headed for the front door, jingling like Santa's sleigh. A couple of assistants followed, leaving the manager to tie up the loose-endy bits with Dad and Fingers.

I wondered if I might be able to squeeze in another leading question about families and missing relatives, and got down hastily from the table to see if I could catch 2thi before he left. But a big black car had appeared silently at the garden gate and 2thi and his minions were getting inside before I had a chance to reopen the conversation.

The manager left soon afterwards, in a car that looked identical to the one 2thi'd driven away in. I was still standing in the porch and staring at its tail-lights as they headed away down the pebbly Wild World road when Tori appeared from the direction of the main gate, her scarf trailing behind her and her cheeks ruddy with the cold and the fresh air.

'Don't tell me Christmas Boy has only just left,' she said, unwinding her scarf and hanging it up.

'How was Cazza?' I asked cautiously.

'Boring,' Tori said. 'Kept asking about you and Tinselpants. I couldn't get her off the subject.'

I suddenly really wanted to be friends with my sister again. I know Cazza'd sworn me to secrecy about 2thi, but Tori was the most sensible person I knew, so I really wanted to share my muddled thoughts somehow, without actually giving Cazza away. I touched her sleeve hopefully.

'Listen, Tor, can I come up to see Koko with you tomorrow morning? I do really want to. I know it seems like I've forgotten about her, but I haven't. Well,' I amended, 'OK, I did for a bit and that's totally my own fault and I'm really really really sorry and you're right to have given me a hard time about it, but I can't stop remembering her now. We could, like, talk on the way maybe?'

Tori folded her arms and looked at me. 'Talk about what?'

'Oh, this and that,' I said, swallowing. 'Stuff. You know.'

'No,' said Tori.

I felt a bit wobbly. 'No, you don't want to talk to me?'

'No, I don't know what "stuff" means,' Tori replied and gave me a cautious smile. 'But you'll explain tomorrow, right?'

18

Wronger Than One Plus Two is Three

'So,' I began as Tori and I walked together towards the medical unit the following morning. 'There's this person. Let's call her . . . Person.'

'With you so far,' said Tori.

'So, Person wants Person Two to ask another person – let's call the other person Person Three – if Person is related.'

'Which person?'

'The first Person,' I explained. 'Person thinks she's related to Person Three, even though it's totally unlikely because they don't look like each other at *all*. But Person is completely convinced and Person Two—'

'Sorry,' said Tori. 'Person Two is . . . ?'

I thumbed myself mutely in the chest. This was still sticking to the 'sworn to silence' rules, right? 'So, as I was saying, Person Two is frankly a bit scared of Person and really wants to give her some good news about being related to Person Three . . .' I stopped, my line of thought as tangled as a ball of wool that's just spent three days with a litter of kittens.

Fortunately – or unfortunately, depending on how you look at it – Tori wasn't tangled at all.

'Cazza thinks she's related to *Tinselpants*?' my sister said in astonishment.

I gaped. 'I didn't tell you that,' I said, once I'd recovered from the shock of Tori's warp-speed thinking. 'Did I? Did I tell you that?'

'It was the bit where you said Person Two is scared of Person,' Tori told me. 'I guessed. It wasn't hard.'

'I didn't say *anything*,' I said anxiously. 'I promised. Got it?'

'I promised not to say anything about the adoption either, so we're quits,' Tori said. 'Of course I won't say that you blabbed. But she actually thinks she's related to Tinselpants? For real?'

I found I didn't mind Tori calling 2thi Tinselpants. His trousers *had* been pretty tinselly.

'No offence, Taya,' Tori added, looking hurt, 'but

why did Cazza tell you and not me?'

'I think she was scared you wouldn't believe her,' I said. 'And as we know, I believe pretty much anything. I'm guessing Cazza didn't want to be laughed at.'

Tori chewed this over for a bit.

'I know it's completely crazy,' I went on, desperate to spill the whole bean casserole now, 'but it's like Cazza's got this hornet in her knickers about being related to the guy. And even though it's completely unlikely – he's blinking *2thi*, for wombat's sake and they don't look at all alike – Cazza might kill me if I go back to her with either no news at all, or just basically bad news that the answer's no. Has she ever said anything about her parents going to Germany?'

'Germany?' said Tori, mystified.

'Tinsel's a German name,' I said. 'I asked 2thi if it was Icelandish or Icelandic or whatever. It was the first place that came to mind. Anyway, he said the name was German. So maybe that's a clue for Cazza to work on and then she'll leave me alone, right?'

Tori's jaw dropped. 'You asked Tinselpants if he was Icelandic? With a name like that, he probably thought you were taking the mickey!'

I clapped my hands to my mouth, aghast. 'I *thought* he looked at me funny!'

Only a doofus like me could come up with an insult and not even realize it might be one!

For once, Tori and I both saw the funny side at the same time. We propped each other up, guffawing into each other's shoulders. I'd basically managed to ask a mega-hard rap star if he was related to Father Christmas!

Koko was sleeping when we got to the unit. She looked very fragile, lying in her cage with bandages wrapped around her middle.

Dr Nik seesawed his big hairy hand at our anxious questions. 'She's very young and the internal injuries were bad,' he said gently. 'We cannot say that she will be fine just yet. But thank you for coming, girls. I am sure Koko would appreciate it if she knew you were here.'

Feeling down, we headed home via the marsupials. What we found there didn't exactly cheer us up.

Even though Tori had warned me, Caramel looked shockingly thin. She was grazing slowly by the marsupial house, but it didn't look like she was eating much. Her coat seemed duller too, although that might have been the cold February light, which can make everything look as grey as itself.

'Is there seriously nothing more you can do to help her?' Tori asked.

'We're trying a new course of food supplements,' Sasha said. Her green hair gave her worried face a sickly glow. 'But if they don't help to bring her weight up, we'll have to go back to the drawing board. I've got to be honest, girls – we're running out of ideas.'

Everything in my life suddenly seemed very clear again. *This* was important – talking to my sister, visiting Koko and trying to figure out how to help Caramel. Rap stars, newspapers and fame were all very well, but they didn't half tire a person out.

On Monday morning, I found that I actually didn't want to talk about 2thi or the music video.

I met my classmates' breathless enquiries about the weekend with basic one- or two-word answers, added more detail when I got some proper questions about Nile crocodiles, and did my best to explain to Jonno Nkobe why I hadn't asked 2thi to autograph my neck. Heather Cashman got quite narky when I tried to change the subject, and she and Carrie slouched off mumbling about me being full of myself, which even I could see was kind of ironic.

'You're late, Catherine,' rapped out Ms Hutson as

Cazza strolled in halfway through the register.

Caz put her hand underneath her jet-black hair and flipped it casually backwards. There was a collective gasp at the massive zigzag that had been shaved into the side of her head, just above her left ear.

'Sorry, miss,' she said, quite plainly not sorry at all. She slid into her normal seat and made a real thing of swishing her hair again. Tori and I got the full zigzag impact right between the eyes.

'Your hair's awesome, Caz!' I said.

'You look like a cat that just had an operation,' Tori said bluntly. 'I know you think you're related to this rapper plonk, but copying his hairstyle won't make it come true.'

Eek. What happened to the 'you won't hear it from me' stuff my sister had spouted on Sunday? If I survived this, I was seriously going to *kill* her!

Cazza's eyes narrowed to tiny slits. She lasered me with her most scary glare.

'I didn't tell!' I squeaked.

'I worked it out for myself,' Tori said. 'Why didn't you tell me, Caz? I wouldn't have laughed.'

For about half a second, Cazza's lip wobbled and her eyes teared up and she didn't look scary at all. And right at that moment I wanted the scary Cazza back because a crying Cazza was wronger than one plus two is three. I mean, four.

Then the moment was gone.

'Yeah, right,' Cazza growled. ''Cause you never laugh at anything I say, do you?'

'I asked about 2thi's family, Caz,' I said quickly, to avoid a full-blown argument. 'On Saturday, when he came.'

Cazza's attention was back on me again, an eagle with a fluffy bunny in its sights. 'Tell me what he said,' she demanded.

'He said his dad was German. His real surname is, um, Tinsel.'

Caz looked a bit thrown. 'I'll be related to his English half then,' she said after a minute. ''Cause there's no way I'm German 'cause I'd, like, speak German, wouldn't I?'

'It's pretty simple, Cazza,' Tori said. 'Talk to your parents. They can help you find your birth family, if that's what you really want.'

Cazza looked at Tori as if she was dirt. 'But they're *not* my parents. A *real* mate would understand that.' The sarky way she said 'real' made Tori flinch. 'Never were, never will be. End of.'

Which I thought was a bit harsh, and it made me

think back to Koko and Caramel. A koala may not be a kangaroo and vice versa, but we had proof that they could love each other just the same, didn't we?

19

Crazed Solo Riff

Cazza was really cold towards Tori for the rest of the day. Tori pretended not to care, but she didn't fool me. I didn't know how to help so I just concentrated on staying alive, deciding that the best way to achieve that was by being as encouraging towards Cazza as I could.

'So when are you shooting the video, babe?' Cazza asked, linking arms with me on the way to English in the afternoon.

'Wednesday,' I said. I shot a look in my twin's direction, but she was chewing the end of her plait and trying to look as if she was listening to what Joe was saying about Warhammer behind us. 'They're shooting the non-crocodile bits of the video in the main part of the day and Dad's driving me up straight after school with Fingers and Toothy for the rest.'

Cazza examined her chewed, black-painted fingernails. 'They doing it in some special recording studio or what?'

'They're filming at a place in Acton in west London called the Wherehouse – spelled WHEREhouse, by the way, because it's a warehouse *where* filming happens, get it?' I told her, grateful that at least I had some concrete facts about the video. 'It's used by loads of bands doing videos, apparently.'

'I'll come with you,' Cazza decided. 'I'll just tell my non-mum that I'm round at yours on Wednesday after school. She won't care.'

I gazed beseechingly at Tori for help. Tori removed her plait from her mouth and took me by the arm.

'It's a closed set,' she said, dragging me out of Cazza's reach. 'We can't invite anyone. Sorry.'

'I wasn't asking *you*, you nerd,' Cazza shouted after Tori. She tried to catch up with us, but got swallowed up by a swarm of Year Nines going the other way. 'And I'm not *anyone*, OK? This is my *family* we're talking about!'

* * *

Fingers was starting to come to the house a lot more, getting Toothy used to the idea that he couldn't be my son for ever. My heart felt a bit funny as I watched the youngster switch his gaze from me to Fingers at feeding time. But when I mentioned this at Fingers's early-morning visit on Wednesday, he rubbed his face with his two-fingered hand and looked me straight in the eye.

'Don't ever kid yourself that you can make friends with a crocodile, Taya. Study them, yes. Enjoy and respect them, sure. But *everything* is prey to a croc. The moment he's big enough, this fella will bite you in half without a second thought. There's a primal brain in there. Hunt or be hunted.'

'Which is why I'm delighted that Mr Tinsel never got back to us about finding a full-grown crocodile for today's shoot,' Dad added. 'Can you imagine the fun we'd all have had?'

'I wouldn't have put it past the man to think he could have one on a dog lead with a wee baseball cap on its head,' said Fingers. 'He didn't seem like the brightest bulb in the chandelier.'

Dad, Fingers and Toothy were going to collect us from school straight after IT that afternoon. Toothy would travel in a special secure box with air holes and padding to stop him banging his delicate little snout during any sharp road-bends or emergency braking, though he would have to do without a swimming pool for a while. Tori was coming too, because Mum had been called to a big afternoon meeting at a wildlife park in Kent and it was basically easier for Dad to have both of us. Tori wasn't completely thrilled about it, but hey.

'You actually might enjoy the music, Tor,' I teased as Tori slowly buckled herself into the van beside me. Dad put his indicator on to pull out into the road with his nose pointing towards London. Beside us on the back seat, Toothy squeaked in a chatty way inside his travel box. 'It's got this thing called a beat and the notes go up and down in a funky pattern.'

'I wanted to spend this afternoon helping Sasha with Caramel,' said Tori.

I stopped teasing immediately and gave her hand a sympathetic squeeze. 'Do you know if Caramel's new supplements are working?'

'I asked Mum for news this morning. She looked really grim, like she'd heard it wasn't working at all.' Tori's eyes were troubled. 'Taya, what if Koko recovers and Caramel's the one who dies?'

Think positive, I instructed myself. As we all know,

I'm pretty good at that. 'That's not going to happen. I promise.'

Tori gazed out of the window and didn't answer.

'Do you know why Caz wasn't in school today?' I asked in a bid to take my sister's mind off her worries.

'Ill, Ms Hutson said,' Tori replied, still staring at the road outside the car.

I pondered this. Cazza had seemed OK yesterday. Bright and glittery, almost. She'd even laughed at one of Joe's attempts at a joke, and it had sounded like she was laughing at the *joke* and not at her more usual target: Joe himself.

Fingers leaned back through the gap between the front seats. 'I'm quite excited about today, girls,' he admitted. 'I used to be in a band myself, you know.'

'Seriously?' I said, impressed. 'What kind of band was it?'

'Thrash metal,' said Fingers. 'Lead guitar.'

He looked wistful, like he was picturing how his life might have been as a hairy thrash-metal guitarist. Fleetingly I wondered if his finger thing wasn't croc-related after all. Perhaps he'd tangled his missing fingers in the guitar strings in a crazed solo riff that went wrong? I decided to try out this exciting theory next time Tori and I played 'How Fingers Lost His Fingers'.

Dad whacked the buttons on the dashboard until he found a rock station and the rest of the journey passed like a flash as we teased Fingers through each song. Even Tori was laughing by the time we swung in to the Wherehouse car park and unloaded ourselves and our little crocodile star.

As we walked towards the main doors, Fingers carrying Toothy's box as tenderly as a baby, Dad's phone buzzed. Whoever was on the other end of the phone was talking both fast and loud. After listening for a little while, Dad covered the receiver with his hand and looked at us.

'It's the mother of your friend Catherine, Tori. She's saying her daughter didn't come home from school and she doesn't know where she is. Did you have any classes with her today?'

20

Da 2th's Da Man!

Tori grabbed the phone.

'Mrs Turnbull? It's Tori, Cazza's friend. Wasn't Cazza ill today? That's what Ms Hutson said. No . . . No, we didn't see her . . .'

Mrs Turnbull's voice came through loud and frightened to all of us, even though Tori was holding the phone close to her ear. It sounded like Cazza's 'illness' was news to her mother.

Fingers shifted Toothy's box to a more comfortable position and tipped his head at the doors of the studio, making the point that we should head inside. Tori passed the phone back to Dad. Her face looked ghostly in the bright lights of the studio car park.

'Mrs Turnbull, we're very sorry not to be able to

help . . .' Dad ushered us towards the studio doors with his free hand. 'There'll be a reasonable explanation . . . Catherine seems like the sort of girl who can, er, look after herself pretty well. Yes, of course . . . No, it seems she said nothing to my daughter about it . . . Let us know if there's anything else we can do.'

He tucked his phone into his pocket. 'It seems that your friend is missing, Tori,' he said soberly.

Tori looked like she was in shock as we filed through the Wherehouse doors. Fingers slid away to fill in the forms at the funky reception desk as Dad did his best to say positive things about an extremely serious situation.

'She disappeared for the afternoon during your Wild World trip, if I remember rightly, and came back safe enough, didn't she? I'm sure this will be no different. Where do you think she might have gone? Did she have friends outside school?'

'She didn't have many friends,' I said. 'Just Tori really.'

'And you're sure she didn't say anything to you yesterday?' Dad checked.

I racked my brains to see if I could come up with anything, but I just hit a series of forbidding brick walls with DANGER! painted on them in blood-red letters.

'She's run away from home,' Tori said. 'She always said she would do it one day. Don't tell me how I know. I just do.'

I shivered. For once, my sister's pessimistic view of the world didn't seem all that unlikely.

A runner in baggy jeans and neon trainers showed us into the huge studio space where 2thi was doing the video. The effect of walking from a cold, dark February afternoon into a thumping world of techno beats, colourful flowers, jungle foliage, with an actual proper *river* somehow twisting across the ground and burning-hot camera lights overhead was totally surreal, but it felt like I was somehow still in the cold car park, frozen in the moment when Dad's phone had rung.

'Are you OK waiting there, Tori love?' Dad pointed at a curtained-off area in the corner of the studio, where through a crack in the curtains I could see a big red sofa and coffee table covered with bottles of juice and water. 'Hopefully this won't take long.'

Tori took her fingers out of her mouth. She'd chewed one of her nails right down to nothing. 'Fine,' she said, sounding tense. 'But can I borrow your phone, Dad?

I'll call everyone I can think of. Someone might know where Cazza's gone. I've got to do *something*.'

We left Tori with Dad's phone and followed our neon-footed runner round the side of the set to a jungle-clearing-type area. 2thi was jigging on the spot with four dancing girls in python-print bikinis wrapped around his arms and legs. Music was pumping through the air and the rapper's pock-marked jaw was working up and down as he mimed to the song like a crazy puppet.

'*Down Wiv U, I'm gettin' Down Wiv U,*
I lurve the fings you do
I'm getting Down Wiv U . . .'

The song may not have had the best lyrics in the world, but the beat was making my bottom twitch from side to side *à la* Shakira. 2thi looked a bit of a twonk in insanely baggy trousers that were heavy with gold chains, a ripped camouflage vest, a belt of machine-gun bullets slung over one shoulder and the usual sunglasses, but he was giving the dancing and the miming thing some serious effort. The girls wriggled and writhed.

Dad exchanged a glance with Fingers and cleared his throat.

'Taya? Why don't you sit over there with Fingers and

Toothy for a minute. This may not, er, be completely appropriate for you . . .'

'It looks like he's being attacked by jungle snakes,' I said, staring at the writhing girls in amazement. 'Ooh! I think that one just bit him!'

'Cut!' shouted someone from behind the cameras.

The music stopped. The dancing girls brushed themselves down, adjusting the strings on their bikinis, comparing blingtastic nail acrylics and tidying up the mad green extensions that had been pinned into their hair. 2thi tucked his camouflage vest back into his trousers and jangled over to us with his golden grin on full display.

'Wassup, crocodile dudes?'

The rapper attempted this complicated high-five routine with Dad – high, low, to the side, round the back of the head. Dad looked very relieved when it was over.

Next up, the director introduced himself. He was a surprisingly ordinary-looking guy with plain brown hair, jeans and a grey T-shirt that looked out of place among all the snakeskin and bling.

'The plan is to have your croc on 2thi's shoulder and zoom in for a real close-up, 2thi looking sideways as he's singing, a bit freaked out that there's a crocodile on his shoulder, bring in a little humour. The shot will only be a couple of seconds long. What do you think? Will that work for you?'

I peeped through one of the breathing holes in Toothy's box. Toothy gazed at me with his usual full-blast intent as Fingers discussed a few safety things with the director. He looked about as relaxed as baby crocs ever get.

2thi threw himself down in a director-style chair with *DON'T MESS WIV DA 2TH* printed on the back. 'Do it, bro,' he said. 'I'm ready. Hey!' he called over to his manager, who was hovering in a bright-green suit in the background. 'Do we sue if this sucker bites me?'

'We have got a contract which means they can't sue us if Toothy bites him, haven't we?' Dad checked with Fingers in a low voice.

When it came down to it, the baby crocodile was a scaly little angel. He sat quietly on the rapper's shoulder with his jaws open in his usual friendly grin, watching me and Fingers to make sure we weren't about to disappear. 2thi mimed just like before, only this time he was sitting totally still and doing all the work with his mouth. The scene was in the can within about five minutes flat. I lifted Toothy off the singer's shoulder and slid him back into his travel box with a combination of relief and triumph. It would have been well embarrassing if Toothy'd bitten his namesake.

'I'm da crocodile man!' crowed 2thi, leaping out of the director's chair and doing a groovy little moonwalk thing the minute Fingers gave the nod. He was clearly just as relieved as I was that he hadn't been gnashed. In fact, he was behaving as if he'd just walked barefoot through a fire pit full of deadly scorpions.

'Da 2th's da man!' shouted someone.

'Da 2th's da man! Da 2th's da man!'

The echo went out across the studio. 2thi's chest swelled up like a camouflaged balloon. 'You ain't seen nothing yet,' he shouted, beating his chest like a small gorilla. He high-fived Dad and Fingers so hard he practically knocked them off their feet. 'We gonna make history today, my friends. You want a croc? I'll give you a croc!'

He did this silly finger snap 'n' click thing at someone, who rushed away into a gloomy corner of the warehouse. And I couldn't help thinking that *he* was the one who'd wanted a croc, not us.

The whole place seemed to be buzzing, nervous and overexcited; a bunch of kids who've eaten too many sweets and suddenly think fighting a cage full of sharks sounds like fun. Something was being wheeled out of the shadows towards the bright camera lights. A long white trailer with a caged door. A pair of ancient, deep-set eyes glittering evilly with reflected light.

2thi punched the air.

'*This*, my friends, is a CROC!'

21

Enwhales and Enseals and Enpenguins

'Meet Killa.' The corners of 2thi's glinting mouth practically met at the back of his head, he was smiling so hard. He did a sort of salute, thumping himself in the chest and pointing at the trailer. 'Killa!'

'Killa!' roared a few of his minions, jumping about and high-fiving and basically behaving like a bunch of orang-utans.

I'd never seen Fingers lost for words before. Killa the fully grown Nile crocodile blinked very slowly at us from the trailer. His teeth glinted in a wicked smile through the bars on the trailer door. I thought about little Toothy in his box. Was he really going to grow into something as terrifyingly enormous as *that*?

Delighted with the effect he was having, the rapper strutted up and down in front of the trailer with quick, stiff little steps like a zigzaggy chicken. The guy was as mad as a bath full of onions.

'Killa! Killa!'

'Do you have a licence for that animal?' Dad demanded, white-faced. 'Why is it here? Where did you get it?'

'I told you at our meeting, bro!' Even though we couldn't see them, I could tell that the rapper's eyes behind his sunnies were bright and triumphant. 'You bring the little guy, I bring the big guy. Man, you look like you gonna drop your guts straight out of your pants!'

The excitable minions guffawed.

'Do you have a licence?' Dad repeated.

Still laughing, 2thi beckoned his manager over. 'Tell the dude, Hans. And hey! Tell him to chill while you're at it.'

'My client has held a Dangerous Wild Animals Licence for three years,' Hans the manager said. 'He has a special facility for his reptiles at a property in Essex. Killa is the crown in his collection. He wishes to showcase the animal in today's shoot.'

'Do we understand this correctly?' Fingers asked,

recovering. 'You plan to use this crocodile in your video today?'

2thi had started doing boxerlike bounces from side to side. 'We doing this today, suckers! Bring it on!'

'Everything has been arranged, yes.' The manager's skinny-fit green suit made him look like a fluorescent runner bean.

'But—' Fingers began.

'This is a professional production, Mr O'Connor,' the manager interrupted smoothly. 'Our director is happy, our technicians are happy, the animal has been checked and is healthy and able to perform. Everything we are doing today complies with regulations regarding animal and personnel safety. The artificial river you see before you has been constructed for this purpose. We have a specially designed underwater cage into which the animal will be lowered and a series of one-way grilles that will control the direction in which it swims until it returns to the original cage, is removed from the water, replaced in the trailer and taken back to Essex. We plan to make something very special here today.'

The way he said this last bit reminded me of a dog with its teeth in a bone. He was basically saying, 'Try and take the bone away and you'll lose another finger, Fingers.'

'Crocodiles have minds of their own,' said Fingers, sounding grim.

'There will be no opportunity for it to think,' the manager assured him. 'It will just swim. You are welcome to stay and watch, but if you feel uncomfortable you can leave at any time. Our business is concluded, to my understanding. Wallis, did you want to reshoot anything with the young crocodile?'

The brown-haired director shook his head. For a 'happy' director, he looked pretty uncomfortable.

'Bring it *on*!' whooped 2thi, who was still bouncing from foot to foot like a trampolining twerp. Why had I ever thought he was cool?

Fingers pulled Dad away from Hans the manager for an urgent conference.

'I think we should stay, Andy. I would feel uncomfortable leaving these idiots unsupervised. Whatever that manager says, these guys don't know crocodiles as well as I do. As there seems no way of persuading them to change the plan, the least I can do is run a few additional checks on the safety equipment, the one-way grilles and the underwater cage. I'm sure they would appreciate a second opinion.'

'I don't think the manager likes opinions,' said Dad. 'But I take your point, Fingers. If something bad happened, I would feel guilty about leaving these people in an unsafe situation. A crocodile took offence at my camera in Africa last year – and it wasn't funny.'

My father'd had a run-in with a wild crocodile? I was suddenly very glad that he didn't do wildlife shoots out in the African bush any more.

Dad's twinkly eyes were serious above his scrubby beard. 'Taya, I don't want you anywhere near the set when that crocodile is released. Take Toothy and join Tori on those red sofas we saw when we came in. She may have some news about your friend.'

I glanced at Killa one more time. It was hard to tell head on, but I guessed he was a good four or five metres long. He made a sudden movement, lunging towards the cage door and banging his snout on the bars, giving everyone a fright. Fingers muttered something under his breath.

'OK,' I said, backing away with Toothy's box clutched tightly to my chest. 'See you later then. Don't, er – don't get too close yourself either, Dad, OK?'

'Believe me, I will be staying well back,' Dad promised.

* * *

Toothy and I found Tori slumped on the red sofa with three empty apple-juice boxes and Dad's phone lying on the coffee table in front of her. She looked so dejected that launching into a breathless account of Killa and the python girls and the whole crazy shebang felt wrong.

'You haven't heard anything else about Cazza, have you,' I said, putting Toothy's box down on the table and collapsing on the sofa beside my sister. 'I can tell from your face.'

'I don't know why I bothered taking Dad's phone,' Tori muttered. 'I didn't know who to call. There's no reason why Joe or Biro would know where Cazza was. I thought of trying to get Heather Cashman's number off Directory Enquiries, but asking for "Heather Cashman, Fernleigh" wasn't going to work, was it? And all these people have been coming in and out making tea and coffee and being all jolly and trying to make conversation with me and all I could think was how Cazza's probably scared and lost and wandering around somewhere out there and I've been no help at all.'

This was a very long speech for Tori and proved how upset she was.

'We have to believe that she's going to be all right,' I said, trying to encourage my twin out of her slump. 'Being negative won't help. It'll just make us feel worse. At least if we stay optimistic, we can fill our brains with endolphins.'

'En*dolphins*?' Tori repeated, puzzled. 'We're not at Sea World.'

'You know, good feelings or chemicals or whatever you call those thingies that zoom around your brain when you're happy,' I said uncertainly.

Tori exploded with laughter. 'En*dorphins*, you nutter!'

'I prefer the sound of endolphins,' I said, grinning through my embarrassment. 'They can join the enwhales and enseals and enpenguins hanging out in the rest of my head.'

Laughter, eh? Doctors ought to go round clinics with clown noses and a book of decent jokes. It may not fix a person's broken leg but a happy person gets well quicker. Fact.

But then . . .

Tori screamed and my heart nearly stopped beating when a head popped up from behind the red sofa. A grinning, black-haired, zigzag-shaved head with a tiny little hole in one nostril.

'Hiya, babes,' said Cazza nonchalantly, hopping over the sofa and landing bang in between us. 'What's the joke?'

22

A Room Full of Daleks

Neither Tori nor I could speak for the shock of seeing Cazza leap into view. It was like that moment when Toothy'd sat on my boot, only not funny.

Cazza spread her arms out along the back of the sofa behind our heads, stretched out her legs and crossed her ankles on the coffee table, where her huge shoes took up half the space. 'Your faces, babes,' she giggled. 'Class.'

'Caz!' croaked Tori. 'You . . . you're here?'

'Got the train this morning. Change of clothes and everything in my bag. Military operation, babes. Seriously. I did this research online about maps and trains and Acton and the Wherehouse – cheers for that, Taya; I'd never have made it if you hadn't said the name of the place – and found a bus timetable to get to this road. I, like, made *notes*!'

She sounded prouder of this fact than the rest put together.

'And there's all these back entrances to this place like you wouldn't believe, so I sneaked in and had a sandwich – yeah, remembered a sandwich, put it right down in my notes – and then there's a little door right behind that curtained bit, like totally designed for sneaking through, babes. And I've been sitting behind this sofa for ages and waiting for all them coffee-making idiots to, like, go away and leave you alone, Tor babes, so I could come out, but they kept not leaving and not leaving and I was getting serious cramp. And then everyone left and Taya came in, so ta-da!'

Cazza laughed again. She was trembly and energized and scarier than ever.

'You left Fernleigh and came here all by yourself?' I said in disbelief. 'But – something could have happened to you! What if you'd got lost, or kidnapped, or knocked over in the traffic or something?'

Cazza seemed disappointed that Tori and I weren't more impressed and pleased to see her. 'You listening or what?' she said, suddenly moody. 'I just *told* you. I did *notes*.'

Tori came to life in spectacular style. 'You total ZONK!' she shouted. 'I can't believe you did this to your mum! To all of us! Take this and call her *right now*' – she practically punched Cazza on the nose as she thrust out Dad's phone – 'or – or – or I'll totally make you wish you were stuck in a room full of Daleks instead!'

Cazza pouted. 'I'm here to see 2thi. And when he sees me, he'll know just the same as I know, that we're *blood*. And no one's gonna spoil it for me – not you, not my non-mum. No one.'

Tori had taken the phone back, her lips pinched and angry. 'Fine. Then I'll call her for you.'

'No!' Cazza made a snatch for the phone, but Tori lifted it out of reach. 'You'll ruin my plan! You'll ruin everything!'

'Call her!' Tori bellowed.

'Never!' Cazza shrieked, trying to wrestle the phone out of Tori's hands. 'I hate you, you cow! I knew you'd try and ruin this for me!'

I threw myself at Tori and managed to grab the phone for myself. Now both my sister and Cazza were screaming at me, their faces angry and twisted.

'Chill out, will you?' I backed away towards the kettle and coffee-maker with the phone behind my back. 'We won't call your mum, Caz, OK? We won't. You won't, will you, Tori?'

'The minute I get that phone,' Tori spat.

'I have to speak to 2thi or everything is *wasted*,' wailed Cazza. 'I'll speak to him and everything will be cool and *then* I'll call! I will!'

'Deal,' I said quickly. I looked at my sister with pleading eyes. 'She just wants to talk to the guy, Tori. When she's seen him we'll call the Turnbulls and everything will be fine.'

Tori's silent nostrils flapped like a raging elephant's ears.

'I'll call,' Cazza insisted, backing towards the curtain that separated our little sofa spot from the rest of the studio. 'I promise. Straight after, yeah?'

And she twisted through the gap and disappeared into the heaving, thumping mass of runners, camera guys, lighting technicians, sound engineers and gigantic jungle trees.

I was still breathing deeply and recovering from the high drama when Tori snatched the phone from me.

'You are *seriously* irresponsible,' she snarled.

Great. More abuse.

'She was about to kill you!' I protested, falling back on the sofa again. 'Bombs need defusing or they blow everyone up. She said she was going to call her mum, OK? We should leave it to her!'

'Humans can feel just as much misery as kangaroos, you know,' Tori snapped. 'Caramel only had Koko in her pouch for a few days and she's practically dying with grief. Mr and Mrs Turnbull have had Cazza for *twelve years*. Can't you make your dim little brain understand that?'

When she put it like that, I felt really bad. How come everything was always so clear for Tori? Right and wrong, black and white. In comparison, my own world was full of grey bits without any edges. Of course Mr and Mrs Turnbull needed to know that Cazza was safe. What had I been thinking of?

Safe. *Safe* . . .

I suddenly got the uneasy feeling that my brain had been trying to tell me something for several minutes. I listened. Then I shot off the sofa like someone had just rammed me with an electric prod. My skin had gone cold, my palms were sweating, my hair literally leaped off my scalp and landed in a tangled heap on the coffee table.

'*Killa!*' I gasped.

There was a fully grown crocodile out in that studio! Dad had ordered me to stay away from the exact place

Cazza'd just rushed off to because it wasn't safe. And I'd just let her go!

'Yes,' agreed Tori, misunderstanding as she lifted the phone to her ear. 'Mrs Turnbull probably *will* kill her. I would. Of all the stupid—'

I squealed and rushed through the curtain, leaving my sister mid-sentence. Wombats! Wombats! No, cut that. Wombats didn't *begin* to cover this level of terror. We were talking great white sharks. We were talking *crocodiles*.

'Excuse me! Excuse me, have you seen . . . ? A girl, black hair . . . Yes, my age . . . Excuse me?'

I slalomed through people carrying rolls of electric cabling, hand-held cameras, chat-chat-chatting like nothing out of the ordinary was going on. No one was helping me and there was no sign of Cazza anywhere.

I skidded round the corner and slammed straight into . . .

'Fingers!' I sobbed with relief.

Fingers looked horrified to see me. 'Taya! Didn't your dad tell you to stay away? We have a situation and you *really* shouldn't be out here.'

He tried to hustle me back the way I'd come. The way he did it was filled with something I'd never sensed in Fingers before.

Fear.

It was suddenly blowing all around me like an evil wind. People began running backwards and forwards with their hands in the air. I was gripped with the most awful feeling of dread.

'Has Killa got her? Cazza?'

Fingers pushed me onwards. 'Who? Please, Taya, just keep moving. We're having to clear the set.'

'Then who?' I said in desperation. 'Killa got Dad?'

'No one's been "got".' Fingers glanced back over his shoulder. 'But there is a problem with the big Nile croc, yes.'

The oilslick of fear was spreading. People had started rushing past us, all aiming for the doors back out to the reception.

'What's happened?' *Cazza* . . .

Fingers's voice was hard. 'One of the set builders decided to add some mud on the bottom of the artificial river. To add jungle authenticity. Well, we've ended up with some jungle authenticity all right. Crocs can be controlled in water up to a point, but the sight of mud trips a switch in a crocodile's brain.

'Killa came out of his cage and tunnelled straight

into the mud. He's gone primal, Taya, and it'll be a heck of a job to catch him again. One false move and someone's going to be lunch.'

23

Strange Parallel Swizzle

'Cazza's back there,' I panted, struggling in Fingers's grasp. 'She just turned up. She wants to meet 2thi and she doesn't know about Killa! I have to find her!'

With a superhuman effort I wrenched myself away and bolted through the sea of people rushing the opposite way. This was *all my fault*. If only I'd made Cazza understand that there was no way she and 2thi could be related. If only I hadn't mentioned the Wherehouse, or been so encouraging, or stopped Tori from phoning Cazza's mum, or let Cazza leave the red-sofa room. Killa's teeth shone in my mind's eye. Someone else grabbed my arm.

'We're going this way, kid,' said the director, trying to tow me back to where I could see Fingers calling and pushing through the crowd towards me. The director looked as grey as his T-shirt, with big black sweat patches under his arms. 'And you will too, if you've got half a brain. There's a crocodile on the loose back there. I can't believe I agreed to this job in the first place!'

I pulled myself free and rushed onwards. The python-bikini girls tottered past, squealing their heads off. The studio was emptying as fast as a glass of Ribena on a hot day. Where it had seemed both gigantic and crowded at the same time when we first arrived, now it just felt gigantic. Some kind of alarm had started ringing, but beneath all that I could hear the whoosh of the river, the water being pumped round in a flowing current. Killa was lurking in that water somewhere. But where was Cazza?

Near the jungle clearing where we'd shot Toothy the croc's scene, 2thi the rapper suddenly appeared. His sunglasses had fallen off and his eyes were staring and crazy. He gave me a shove, desperate to get past me and run for safety, but the gold chains that decorated his baggy trousers caught on a bit of jungle greenery and he was pulled to a halt right beside me, swearing his head off. I grabbed him by the front of his vest, hoping that the bullet belt slung around his chest wasn't real and about to start exploding.

'My friend is here somewhere! She came especially to meet you. Have you seen her? Did she find you?'

2thi batted me off with a shriek and tugged at his jewellery. His shaking hands made a total mess of it and he ended up getting more tangled in the greenery than ever. I thought of Rabbit getting stuck in her bush. She'd been a sight more dignified about it than this idiot.

'HANS, MAN!' the rapper bawled, pulling helplessly at the knot of chains and twigs and leaves that was holding him in place as his manager dashed into view. 'Get me out of here. And someone get this dumb kid out my way! I'm too young to die!'

Hans looked calmer than his blubbing client, but his face was as green as his suit. He gripped 2thi under the arms and pulled, with 2thi sobbing like a baby the whole time.

'That Killa – he's a killer, man! Like, a killer!'

'Shut up, you fool,' Hans snarled. He snapped his head round to me. 'Help me here, will you?'

I grabbed 2thi's arms and helped Hans to heave. Jungle greenery and trousers were locked in battle for about five seconds of grunting and weeping before the bush won and 2thi's trousers ripped completely off his legs. I'm sorry to report that his pants had a python-skin pattern on them, with DA 2TH written in gold on the rapper's backside.

'Taya!'

Dad's scruffy head appeared in my line of sight, heading towards me with Fingers close behind. But he would have to wait. I still hadn't got the answer I needed from 2thi.

'Come on, Tinselpants,' I demanded. 'Have you seen my mate or not?'

But I was caught up in Dad's arms and hugged half to death before the rapper could stop sobbing long enough to answer.

'Taya! If I weren't so relieved, I would be yelling at you so loudly right now that your ears would get blown halfway to Africa. What do you think you're *doing*? I *told* you—'

'Not now, Dad!' I interrupted. 'Cazza's here and I have to . . .'

On the far side of the river – the one with the fully grown, primal, hungry crocodile in it – I suddenly glimpsed a flash of movement. My brain did a strange parallel swizzle. This was the exact same feeling I'd had back the first time I saw Koko in Caramel's pouch.

Cazza was moving steathily through the trees and

trying not to be seen. Normally an all-black ensemble is good camouflage if you're sneaking around, but just at that moment she had chosen to inch past a bright-green tree covered in red flowers the size of dinner plates and the black wasn't blending in.

'There!' I shouted.

Dad gasped. Fingers froze. 2thi kept crying.

Cazza saw me pointing. She gave a shrug like she'd been expecting it, walked to the edge of the river and stuck her hands in the air.

'OK, you got me,' she said with a smirk. 'Took you long enough.'

The river whooshed and pumped by her feet. Pleased to have everyone's attention, she sauntered towards the little rope bridge that had been built over the water.

'Turn the alarms off, will you? I ain't burgling nothing. I just wanted to see 2thi, have a little chat. You're a legend, man!' she called, her eyes brightening as she clocked the rapper. 'I totally love you, you know? I love you more than a fan – like, way more! I know this sounds crazy, but I got this feeling deep down . . .'

She took in the fact that her hero/relative was blubbering in his manager's arms, python pants on display, and stopped.

'Whoa,' she said after a moment. 'Those kecks are *gross*.'

I wish I could say there was a slow-motion moment when Killa flew out of the river with his jaws open wide. I wish I could describe every droplet of water as it surged up in a mighty spray of diamonds, the terror of the moment turned into some mega wildlife show for an HD channel. I heard Tori's voice from long ago – *Dawn, and the animals in the jungle are stirring* . . . But everything else was a blur of screaming, a wash of water and a glint of wet mud-brown scales.

It was only afterwards that I understood how Fingers had hurled himself on top of the crocodile and pinned it firmly to the ground with his knees behind its front legs and slammed its mouth shut with both hands. Apparently crocodiles have an astonishingly powerful bite, but the muscles they use to open their mouths to begin with are weak and weedy – something I won't be testing out for myself any time soon.

2thi screamed like an opera diva and fainted. Cazza screamed as well, more understandably. What the heck, I joined in. Seeing Fingers wrestling with Killa on the bank of the artificial river was one memory that was going to take a long time to leave my brain.

'Rope!' shouted Fingers, holding Killa's jaws shut as

Dad rushed in and pulled Cazza out of the way. The crocodile thrashed around angrily but seemed unable to throw Fingers off. 'And when he's secure, we need four or five people to lift him back into his cage. Now!'

Hans, the manager, dropped the zonked 2thi to the ground and rushed to find rope. When he returned, he was accompanied by four burly blokes all looking extremely scared. Dad pushed a shellshocked Cazza at me.

'Look after her,' he ordered, and ran over to help Fingers bind Killa's jaws with the rope.

Someone pressed a button to lift Killa's cage out of the river – the cage he was supposed to have swum back into before being loaded on to the trailer and taken home. The four burly men stood well back until they were satisfied that the croc's teeth were out of action and then stepped in to heft the beast off the ground and stash him safely in the cage. The door was shut and locked and the rope round Killa's jaws was taken off. Behind bars once again, Killa glared at the world.

'I need a cup of tea,' said Fingers shakily. Dad clapped him hard on the back and half a dozen other people attempted to shake his hand. 'Can someone put the kettle on?'

Cazza flung two trembling arms around me in a very unCazza-ish way. 'Croc . . . croc . . . croc . . .' she wept.

'I know,' I soothed as best I could, given that I was still having trouble breathing. 'But it's OK now. You're safe. It's over.'

Cazza put her head back with a wail of misery. 'I . . . want . . . my MUM!'

For a moment, I actually believed in magic. What other explanation could there possibly have been for the sudden and miraculous appearance of Mrs Turnbull herself, coming across the studio floor towards us at a run, slightly less immaculate than usual in a crumpled grey shirt and cream skirt combo with her dark hair tumbling over her eyes, leaping over 2thi (still out cold on the floor) to pull Cazza into a hug? My jaw sagged open. It was *amazing*. It was *incredible*. It was—

'I phoned her, you twerp,' Tori panted, running into my line of vision and reading my gobsmacked face with her usual accuracy. 'It wasn't hard.'

24

The Swede Spot

Mrs Turnbull had traced Cazza as far as Acton by
checking the history on Cazza's computer and finding
maps and bus timetables. Then she'd gone to Fernleigh
station and asked the ticket guy if he remembered
selling a ticket to Acton to Caz – which he did, Cazza
being a noticeable sort of girl. Finally she'd whizzed
like a racing driver up the M3. Tori's phone call had
caught her somewhere around Hammersmith. So it
was magic that had brought her to the Wherehouse so
quickly, but magic of the kind which makes an elegant
person with nice clothes and a busy job cancel
important meetings, yell at teachers, demand results
from police and generally behave like a slavering
bloodhound chasing its quarry. What's that magic

called again? Oh yes – motherhood. If it had been me or Tori who'd vanished, I knew Mum would have done just the same, only with more shouting and clothes covered in dog hair.

'Mrs Turnbull's really nice,' I commented as Dad swung us all back through the Wild World gates at eight o'clock that evening. 'I don't see why Cazza is always so horrible about her.'

'Mr and Mrs Turnbull should have told Caz about her adoption sooner,' said Tori.

'They probably regret that,' I said, thinking back to Mrs T's tearstained face at the Wherehouse.

'Maybe they didn't tell her because they didn't want it to be true,' said Tori. 'Stupid, but a tiny bit understandable if you love someone like your own child.'

We both fell quiet until Dad had parked the van round the back of our house. Fingers flipped off his seatbelt and opened the passenger door, blasting us all with freezing air.

'Tor?' I said.

'Yes,' Tori agreed. 'I want to go and see Caramel too.'

We left Toothy with Dad and Fingers and headed straight back into the park. The floodlights along the pathways made our shadows very long and black on the pebbled track.

'Sasha and Paul have probably gone home,' I said. I snuggled my chin deeper into my coat. 'It's late.'

Tori pointed to the glow in the dark air above the marsupial enclosure. 'It may be late, but it looks like they're still here.'

'Do you think that's good or bad?' I asked nervously.

Tori answered by speeding up. I broke into a nervous jog beside her; she ran faster still. By the time we reached the marsupials we were at a full-stretch sprint. We could see Sasha illuminated in the window of the marsupial-keepers' office. Panting and holding her side, Tori knocked at the window for Sasha's attention.

'How . . . are Caramel's supplements . . . working?' I gasped when Sasha opened the door to let us in.

'Not as well as we would like,' Sasha admitted. 'Paul and I are monitoring her through the night – I'm on the first shift. Thanks for coming, guys. Do you want to see her?'

Caramel was hunched in a little stall inside the marsupial house. We could see her shoulder bones sticking up through her fur. She looked completely wretched, her food untouched beside her. I felt Tori's hand creep into mine and squeeze.

'She's pining for Koko,' I said as powerful emotions fluttered around inside my chest like injured butterflies at the sorry sight. 'She's desperate to see her baby, Sasha. Just like Mrs Turnbull.'

Sasha looked confused.

'It's a long story,' Tori put in. 'And we'll tell you about it some other time. When is Koko going to leave the unit and come back here?'

'Not for a while yet,' said Sasha. She wiped her face with the back of her hand in a defeated sort of way.

'Hey!' I said as an idea bonked me square between the eyes. 'Can't Dr Nik have Caramel as an overnight guest up at the unit? Perhaps if she can spend time with Koko, she'll find a bit of spirit again.'

Sasha's worry lines lifted. 'That's an extremely good idea,' she said in wonder. 'We were on the verge of calling Dr Nik anyway. He wouldn't normally put two animals of different species in the same recuperation cage, but I can certainly ask. You might have hit on the answer!'

'Nice one, Taya,' Tori said in admiration as Sasha rushed for the phone in the office. 'Seriously.'

I glowed at my twin's praise. A proper glow, not a big-headed one. I was reminded of all the important stuff, all over again. It's hard to explain, but Sasha's sudden hope and my sister's smile hit my soul in a completely different place to all the crazy, exciting stuff of the previous week. I think it's called the swede spot, though I've probably got that wrong.

Sasha came back, rubbing her hands. 'He'll be down in a few minutes. Who wants to help me box Caramel up?'

The little kangaroo was featherlight. She didn't resist as we lifted her carefully into a travelling cage and prepared her for the short trip up the hill to the unit. Then we helped Sasha carry the cage outside.

It wasn't long before Dr Nik's headlights swung around the corner from the unit. We helped to slide Caramel's cage into the back of his car and buckled it securely into place. Then, at Dr Nik and Sasha's insistence, we squeezed into the back seat and set off up to the unit – all together.

'Koko's a lot better,' Dr Nik told us as he drove. 'I checked her stitches just this afternoon and they're healing well. A couple more days to be absolutely sure there's no secondary infection, and we'll have her back with her mother soon after that.'

'Caramel's her mother,' I said, glancing at the motionless little kangaroo in the back.

Dr Nik smiled. 'So let's see what the power of

motherly love can do to heal Caramel's broken heart, shall we?'

In the unit, Koko was awake and walking around her spacious recuperation cage, although her bandages got in the way a bit. She wasn't moving very fast, but she was looking much better. Bigger too. Her big brown eyes were bright and her tufty ears flicked with interest as we carried Caramel's cage towards her.

Caramel stirred and twitched her soft, flexible nose.

'She can smell Koko!' said Tori.

Sasha lifted the kangaroo from her cage and placed her inside the recuperation cage with the little koala. There was a pause. Caramel took two slow hops towards Koko, her nose woffling like crazy – as if she'd just smelled the most delicious rose in the world, or the warmest freshest loaf of bread at the baker's.

The next bit happened so fast, we almost missed it. Koko's bandages snagged a little on the edge of Caramel's pouch, but she scrambled in and disappeared from sight. Caramel's shoulders dropped and she made a clucking sound like a contented and rather sleepy chicken. Her baby was home.

'You couldn't make it up,' said Dr Nik, grinning at us. 'Could you?'

A wet-eyed Sasha passed me and Tori a couple of

tissues. I mopped an emotional bogey off the end of my nose.

Yup. Motherhood was magic for sure.

25

Old Scaly Sock

It was time to say goodbye to Toothy, who was heading over to join his sister in the tropical house.

Tori and I both hung over the end of the bannister, watching as Fingers helped Mum dismantle Toothy's temporary fish tank and load the baby croc into the same little wooden travelling box that he'd used for his moment of musical history.

'You aren't too sad about this, are you, girls?' asked Dad anxiously.

'Don't ask me,' said Tori. 'He's Taya's baby.'

'Honest answer?' I said as everyone looked at me. 'Every time I look at Toothy now, I think of how he'll turn into Killa some day – and while that's totally natural for him, it's a bit freaky for me. You know that beady look he does at you, when he doesn't blink for ages? I don't actually know any more if he wants me to give him food or *be* food.'

Fingers slid the lid on to Toothy's travel box and pressed it down. 'If you decide to work with reptiles in the future, Taya,' he said, 'that thought may save your life one day.'

'On the subject of Killa,' said Dad conversationally, 'Hans, Nigel Tinsel's manager, called just now. Guess what?'

'Tinselpants is bringing out a range of tinsel pants especially for Christmas,' Tori said promptly. 'Python-skin ones with gold writing on them.'

'Mr Tinsel doesn't want Killa any more,' said Dad as I giggled helplessly at the memory of Tinselpants's pants. 'In fact, he's selling his entire reptile collection. No one wants Killa though – oddly enough.'

'That's terrible!' gasped Mum. 'This poor animal has done nothing and he will be cast out like an old scaly sock? What is *wrong* with this Tinsel man?'

Hello? This was a man-eating monster we were talking about here, Mum, not a helpless furry infant!

'I thought you might feel that way, Anita love,' said Dad. 'I suggested to Hans that he give either Fingers or Matt a call. If you're serious about developing the reptile side of your research here at Wild World, I can't imagine a better starting point than a fully grown Nile crocodile, can you?'

Oh boy.

'Well,' said Tori into the silence, 'the first thing you have to do is to change that poor animal's name to Kill*er*. E-R, like the proper word.'

'Actually, I've always wanted a crocodile called Claude,' Fingers said with excitement. 'So we'll call him that. It'll be a fresh start. Claude the croc has a ring to it, don't you think?'

Mum whooped and did a little jig with Fingers round the kitchen table. Dad turned the radio on to a cheery song and started conducting, waving the film script he was clutching like a papery baton.

'Mad,' Tori muttered to me. 'The lot of them. Totally insane.'

'Fingers?' I demanded. 'Do you actually *want* to lose another finger?'

Fingers stopped dancing. 'I didn't lose my fingers to a crocodile, you know,' he said breathlessly. 'I was just born this way. Who's for the next dance, then?'

with Lucy Courtenay ...

Q) Where did you get your inspiration for the WILD books?

A) My inspiration for the WILD books started with an abiding interest in the Harry Potter film owls. Where did the director get them from? How do you train owls? Despite their reputation for wisdom, an owl's large and amazing eyes take up so much room in its skull that its brain is actually pretty weedy. I happily imagined classrooms full of owls, learning how to swoop into shot on cue and deliver parcels with perfect accuracy. And then I thought how much fun it would be to come up with a family who have an animals-on-film business. I would have them visiting film sets and video shoots, learning about different animals as they went along and having mad animal-related adventures that their schoolmates could only dream about. Bingo, WILD was born!

Q) Are you more like Tori or Taya?

A) I think I'm more like Tori than Taya. I like to know everything before I make decisions, I am overly serious sometimes, I can be quick and sarcastic, I generally make sensible decisions and I was good at school. However, there are plenty of Taya bits in me too. I am easily distracted, I'm naturally optimistic, I know more about popular culture and famous people than I should, I love fashion, I talk too much and I can be scatty . . .

Q) What's your favourite kind of animal?

A) My favourite kind of animal is probably something soft and fluffy, particularly if it's a baby. Cats are a big thing with me: tigers, snow leopards, my own rather fat and bad-tempered tabby Crumble. But I recently saw some real live elephants for the first time, and was completely amazed by them. And you can't really describe an elephant as soft and fluffy, can you? Uh-oh. Some Taya indecisiveness creeping in here. I think as long as it's not a wasp, I'm pretty happy.

Q) What were your favourite books as a child?

A) My favourite books? Willard Price's ADVENTURE series had me completely engrossed from the age of seven. I learned about spitting cobras and poisonous jellyfish, clever dolphins and mighty tigers, huge anacondas and blue-tongued polar bears and magnificent whales and . . . Mind you, I loved stories about magic and school too. Enid Blyton and The Hardy Boys adventures were favourites, as were Tintin and Asterix books. Oh wombats! How is a person supposed to choose? Tori would know the answer to this one straight away. So perhaps I'm more of a Taya after all!

WILD

ON THE WEB

If you're mad about Lucy Courtenay's WILD series
then visit the Hodder Children's Books website.
Here you'll find news and reviews, as well as
exclusive competitions and sneak peeks at other
books in the series.

www.hodderchildrens.co.uk/wild